Backwoods Romeo

by **John Nash**

Revised by **J.C. Mullen**

Single copies of plays are sold for reading purposes only. The copying or duplicating of a play, or any part of play, by hand or by any other process, is an infringement of the copyright. Such infringement will be vigorously prosecuted

Baker's Plays
7611 Sunset Blvd.
Los Angeles, CA 90046
bakersplays.com

NOTICE

This book is offered for sale at the price quoted only on the understanding that, if any additional copies of the whole or any part are necessary for its production, such additional copies will be purchased. The attention of all purchasers is directed to the following: this work is fully protected under the copyright laws of the United States of America, the British Commonwealth, including Canada, and all other countries of the Copyright Union. Violations of the Copyright Law are punishable by fine or imprisonment, or both. The copying or duplication of this work or any part of this work, by hand or by any process, is an infringement of the copyright and will be vigorously prosecuted.

This play may not be produced by amateurs or professionals for public or private performance without first submitting application for performing rights. Royalties are due on all performances whether for charity or gain, or whether admission is charged or not. Since performance of this play without the payment of the royalty fee renders anybody participating liable to severe penalties imposed by the law, anybody acting in this play should be sure, before doing so, that the royalty fee has been paid. Professional rights, reading rights, radio broadcasting, television and all mechanical rights, etc. are strictly reserved. Application for performing rights should be made directly to BAKER'S PLAYS.

No one shall commit or authorize any act or omission by which the copyright of, or the right to copyright, this play may be impaired. No one shall make any changes in this play for the purpose of production.

Publication of this play does not imply availability for performance. Both amateurs and professionals considering a production are strongly advised in their own interest to apply to Baker's Plays for written permission before starting rehearsals, advertising, or booking a theatre.

Whenever the play is produced, the author's name must be carried in all publicity, advertising and programs. Also, the following notice must appear on all printed programs, "Produced by special arrangement with Baker's Plays."

Licensing fees for BACKWOODS ROMEO is based on a per performance rate and payable one week in advance of the production.

Please consult the Baker's Plays website at www.bakersplays.com or our current print catalogue for up to date licensing fee information.

Copyright © 1947 by Walter H. Baker Company
Made in U.S.A.
All rights reserved.

BACKWOODS ROMEO
ISBN 978-0-87440-672-6
2028-B

STORY OF THE PLAY

Can you imagine a young man, over twenty-one, who has never seen or talked to a girl? Well, Romeo Montague was in that predicament. His parents died when he was a child and his uncle, a scientist, took him into the wilds of Canada, one hundred miles from nowhere, where he reared and educated the boy. Larry McNeil and Rex Simonds, two young Americans on a hunting trip, ran across Romeo just after his uncle had died and asked him to visit them in the States. To keep him out of trouble on the trip they arranged for an airplane to bring him to the airport and a taxi to bring him to their home, so the young man arrived at the McNeil establishment still unacquainted with women. BUT—in the McNeil household were Connie and Billie, Larry's sisters, two young ladies who were anything but shrinking violets. There was also a Spanish maid, La Reina, and Orpha, the girl Larry expected to marry, to say nothing of young and vivacious Aunt Rachel. Nor can we overlook the Amazon Queen of the furniture movers and her four helpers who come to repossess the McNeil furniture at the most inopportune times. Romeo was young, handsome, and unspoiled, and all the women fell for him and how! Along with Romeo's problem of adjusting himself to his altered condition in life, Larry was having trouble collecting his inheritance, which came to him solely on condition that he bring before the world some noted scientific discovery and Larry was about as much of a scientist as Romeo was a ladies' man. There was also the problem of the furniture on which the McNeils owed some money, as well as a smashed auto which Rex borrowed and wrecked. All these problems piled together kept the McNeil home in an uproar for days, when, of all people, Romeo adjusted them.

BACKWOODS ROMEO

CHARACTERS

LARRY MCNEIL, *head of the McNeil household.*
REX SIMONDS, *Larry's would-be brother-in-law.*
ROMEO MONTAGUE, *the " backwoods Romeo."*
CONNIE MCNEIL, *Larry's eldest sister.*
BILLIE MCNEIL, *Larry's kid sister.*
ORPHA FINLEY, *a pretty bit of " heart balm " for Larry.*
RACHEL MCNEIL, *the McNeils' young aunt.*
LA REINA, *the maid, a Barcelona bombshell.*
SUE, *the insurance agent.*
FOREWOMAN, *the " boss's " right-hand woman.*
FOUR HELPERS, *women furniture movers.*

ACT I.   Five o'clock, a summer afternoon.

ACT II.   Same time, the following afternoon.

ACT III.   The same time a few evenings later.

SCENE: Living-room of the McNeil summer home, Northern New York.

STAGE DIAGRAM

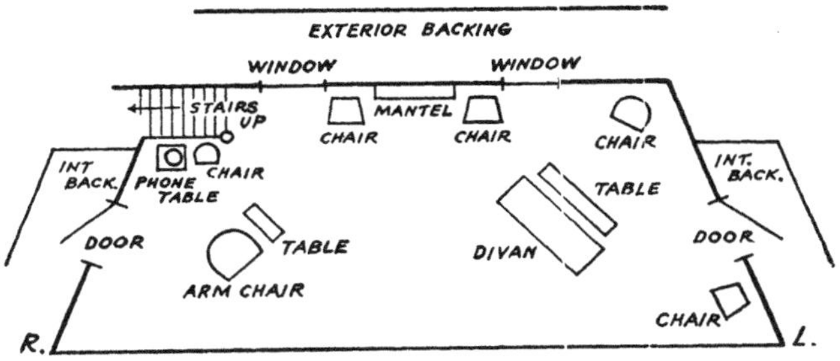

Windows and mantel not necessary for producing play.

STAGE PROPERTIES

Two tables.
Telephone (not absolutely necessary).
Six small chairs.
Large easy armchair.
Divan.
Rugs.
Curtains.
Cushions.
Books.
Magazines.
Ornaments for mantel.

PERSONAL PROPERTIES

Broom.
Bomb.
Bandana handkerchief.
Brief case.
Legal paper.
Characters and costumes described at point of entrance.
The part of Romeo should be played by a strong, husky
young man, rather naive but decidedly not effeminate.

Forewoman should be played by a large, husky girl, one
who will give the impression she is able to handle herself
in all emergencies.

Full lights for all three acts.

BACKWOODS ROMEO

ACT I

Scene.—*The room is well furnished in a manner denoting good financial circumstances on the part of the McNeil family. Door* R. *leads to the outside, door* L. *to the library. Stairs in upper* R. *corner of room lead to the upstairs. There is a small landing at the foot of stairs. A small table and chair, with telephone, is placed in* R. *corner before stairs. Pencil and papers are on the table. Back* C. *is a large fireplace and mantel with candle holders and sundry other articles. On either side of the fireplace is a window with curtains. Between the windows and fireplace are two occasional chairs. A large divan is placed across* L. C. *of room, with book table back of it, and armchair to match, with small book table, is placed* R. C. *Carpet and rugs on floor, with appropriate pictures and electrical fixtures, complete the room.*

(It is five o'clock in the afternoon and the room is empty when curtain rises. Then doorbell or buzzer sounds insistently from off R. *In a moment* La Reina, *the McNeil maid, enters from stairs. She is a pretty Spanish girl in her early twenties wearing a spick and span maid's uniform. She hurries down the stairs and goes to door* R. La Reina *speaks with an accent but it is recommended that the one playing the role merely suggest this accent by using the broad vowel sounds. "It," "this" or "his" should be given the double EE sounds as "eet," "thees" and "hees." If this is done the stilted manner in which the speeches are written will gain the desired effect.)*

LA REINA. (*At door*) What is it you want?

FOREWOMAN. (*Brushes* LA REINA *aside and enters*) We've come for the furniture. (*The* FOREWOMAN *is a large domineering woman, dressed in coveralls and wears a visor 'for a hat. Her four assistants immediately follow her into the room. It is difficult to describe them individually as they all wear baggy coveralls and little paint caps, the only feminine touch about them being their hair. They always walk, act and move as one person. On their entrance they immediately cross to fireplace as though to pick it up.*) Not the fireplace, dummies! That's nailed down. We want the sofa, armchair, table and —— (*Looks around.*) Oh, yes! Them two occasional chairs there. Now snap it up; it's about quittin' time.

(*The four cross to chairs and divan where they stand.*)

LA REINA. (*Facing the* FOREWOMAN) But for why?

FOREWOMAN. (*Scathingly*) Listen, sister! My company ain't in business for its health. We sell household compliances and we expect to get the old mazuma in return for them.

LA REINA. (*Questioningly*) Maz-mazuma?

FOREWOMAN. You know! Boodle!

LA REINA. Boodle? Why for you say boodle?

FOREWOMAN. Filthy lucre then. How does that strike you? There's still a hundred and fifty smackers due on this stuff and it's been due for some time.

LA REINA. (*Still at sea*) Smackers? You—you mean kisses?

FOREWOMAN. (*Disgustedly*) Kisses? Forget it! The furniture ain't *paid* for and that's why we're gonna drag it out. Come on, girls! Grab the divan! We'll take it first. (*The helpers cross two to each end of divan ready to work but each time a conversation begins they stop and stand watching the* FOREWOMAN.)

LA REINA. (*Excitedly*) No! (*Rushes to divan as though to protect it.*) My goodness! My gracious!

(*Starts for stairway.*) Miss Connie! (*She runs slap-bang into the* Forewoman, *almost knocking her over.*)

Forewoman. (*Angrily*) Say! Look where you're goin'!

La Reina. (*Still very much excited*) I go where *I* look but you no look where I go! (*Drags* Forewoman *to door* l.) Mister Larry! Senor! Mister Larry! The muebles! The furniture! She is going while I look.

(Rex Simonds *enters* r. *He is a well-dressed young man with an engaging personality and a beaming smile. He stops in amazement at* La Reina *and the* Forewoman *and the four helpers.*)

Rex. Well! What gives?

La Reina. Oh, Mister Rex! (*She starts for* Rex *and again almost knocks the* Forewoman *off her feet.*)

Forewoman. What is this? Every time I turn around I have to shed that skyrocket.

La Reina. Always you look where I don't go.

Rex. (*As* La Reina *again starts for him*) What's wrong, Queenie? What in heck's going on?

La Reina. Oh, Senor Rex! You are such a sore sight for my eyes!

Rex. (*To* Forewoman) What in thunder is that bunch of penguins doing with the divan?

La Reina. (*As* Forewoman *attempts to speak*) Oh, Senor Rex! They take him away!

Rex. Yeah?

Forewoman. Yeah! No money—no furniture! Get it?

Rex. But Larry'll pay you.

Forewoman. That ain't what I was told by my boss, brother.

Rex. I don't give two hoots what your boss-brother told you! That furniture stays here.

La Reina. (*Nodding violently*) Si! Si! She stay!

Rex. (*To* La Reina) Where's Larry?

La Reina. I think in the library. I yell but I not dare to leave.

REX. (*To* FOREWOMAN) Relax and keep your cover-alls on, sister. (*Crossing to door* L.) We'll dig up something.

FOREWOMAN. (*Stopping him*) Nothing but a payment of do-ray-me'll keep that furniture here. (*To helpers.*) O. K., girls! Wait a minute until we see what plump Percy digs up!

(*The girls immediately sit on divan like penguins.*)

REX. O. K., pickle-puss Polly! I'll be right back.

[*Exits* L.

(BILLIE MCNEIL, *the youngest member of the family, enters stairs. She is a pert little thing of nineteen, dressed in slacks and sports shirt. She stops and stares curiously at scene below.*)

BILLIE. My goodness! Why didn't someone tell me that everyone was going to wear formals?

(FOREWOMAN *glares at* BILLIE *as* LA REINA *rushes to meet her at foot of stairs.*)

LA REINA. Oh, Miss Billie! (*Pointing dramatically at* FOREWOMAN.) She say no dinero, no muebles!

BILLIE. No money, no furniture? (LA REINA *nods violently.*) Well! (*Exits stairs calling.*) Connie! Connie!

FOREWOMAN. (*To* LA REINA) For the size of you, you can sure stir up more trouble than an atomized bomb!

LA REINA. I should spray the furniture with DDT and then it would not have the termites.

FOREWOMAN. (*Rolling up her sleeves*) Who's a termite? Why, you Barcelona bombshell! I'd oughta——

(LARRY *enters* L. *He is a well set up young man of twenty-five, neatly dressed.* LARRY *possesses that obvious confidence which may be associated with one who has always had money at his command—although he hasn't now.*)

Larry. What's this I hear about the furniture?

(*The* Forewoman *turns to face* Larry *just as* La
Reina *also rushes for him. They collide again.*)

La Reina. (*As she hits the* Forewoman) Ugh!
Cow!
Forewoman. (*Angrily*) Who's a cow?
La Reina. Again you no look where I go. (*To*
Larry.) Oh, Mister Larry! She say no dinero, no
muebles. I mean, no smackers, no furniture.
Larry. (*Puts* La Reina *aside and speaks to* Fore-
woman) What's all this about?
Forewoman. That there mobile atom bomb's already
told you all that I got to say. No money, no furniture!
That's my company's motter!
Larry. But can't you understand that I have an in-
heritance coming up and as soon as it's ——
Forewoman. (*Scornfully*) Sure! We know all
about that. The boss told me that you'd got to make some
scientific discovery before you could get your breadhooks
on your Dad's fortune and that, as a scientist, you'd make
a very good bricklayer.
Larry. (*Reasonably*) I know to the average layman
the idea of a scientific discovery sounds insurmountable
but Dad didn't specify any particular type of discovery.
He merely stated that in order to claim my inheritance I
must contribute to the field of scientific research and I intend doing it.
Forewoman. (*Impatiently*) Listen, Mr. McNeil!
My company and you've gone ring-around-rosy with that
deal a dozen times. Now we sell household compliances
and we give terms. If them there terms ain't met, why,
we just take 'em back, the compliances I mean.
Larry. Won't you try to understand that I'll have all
kinds of money in a very short time?
Forewoman. When?
Larry. I can't state any specific time but ——
Forewoman. What you call a little while and what we
call a little while is two horses of different colors. (*Ges-*

turing to the helpers.)   Come on, girls, we gotta get this stuff outta here.

REX.   (*Races through door* L. *with a broom clutched in his hand*)   WATCH OUT!   There he goes!   (*He rushes toward fireplace, whacking violently on the floor with broom.*)   Oooops, there he is!   (*Races to back of divan.*)   Hey!   Come on, you guys!   Help me catch this mouse.

(*At mention of the word " mouse," LA REINA gives a piercing scream and jumps up on armchair* R. C.   *The* FOREWOMAN *suddenly drops her mannish swagger and races for door* R.   *The four helpers give forth with very undignified squeals of terror and in unison dash out door* R. *in the wake of the charging* FOREWOMAN *as* CONNIE *and* BILLIE *appear on the landing to see the cause of the commotion.*)

LARRY.   (*As the furniture movers disappear through door* R.)   Rex!   Lock the outside door!   La Reina! Lock the French windows in the library!

LA REINA.   (*Shuddering*)   No!   No!   NO!   *Raton!*

REX.   (*Hurrying toward door* R.)   There wasn't any mouse, Queenie.   I just faked it.   (*He locks outside door.*)

LARRY.   (*Helping* LA REINA *from chair*)   Quick! There wasn't any mouse.   Rex pulled that act to scare them out.   Lock the French windows in the library, quickly!

LA REINA.   (*As she hurries* L.)   Si!   Si!   No raton! I lock the French windows.   [*Exits* L.

CONNIE (*Speaking from landing*)   What in the world has been going on here?   Billie's been babbling wildly about someone taking the furniture.   (CONNIE *is an attractive girl in her twenties.   She is wearing a pretty dressing gown over an attractive house dress.*)

BILLIE.   (*As she and* CONNIE *come down stairway*) Those women were going to take it, weren't they, Larry?

LARRY.   (*Grumbling*)   That furniture company is worrying because my inheritance hasn't come through yet and they want their money *now*.   When I get ——

CONNIE. But you really don't know a thing about science, Larry.

LARRY. I know that but I'll run across someone who does know something about it. I think I have right now, as a matter of fact.

BILLIE. (*With eager interest*) Have you, honest?

REX. Boy-oh-boy! Did that act of mine move the furniture movers! (*Crosses to divan* L. C.) And there wasn't any mouse at all. Was that a joke on them!

LARRY. (*Laughing*) I'll hand it to you, Rex. You surely had your wits about you that time.

REX. What do you mean? I always have my wits —— (*Suddenly a surprised look crosses his face and he slaps his hand on his right knee.*) HOLY CATS! I didn't fake it! There was a mouse! It's up my pants leg!

LARRY. Are you trying to kid US?

REX. (*As he hops toward door* L.) NO! I've got him and he's got me! Holy cats!   [*Exits* L.

(*They all laugh heartily.*)

CONNIE. (*To* LARRY) What did you mean when you said a moment ago you thought you had found someone who does know about science?

BILLIE. Yes, tell us. Is there a chance that we really may get the inheritance?

LARRY. Remember Rex and me telling you that we had a surprise in store for you, when we returned from our trip last week?

CONNIE. Of course, but what in the world did you find away up in the Canadian woods?

BILLIE. He's kidding us. I know him. They admitted they were over a hundred miles from civilization.

LARRY. (*Smugly*) You'd be surprised at *what* and *who* we found.

REX. (*Enters* L., *all smiles*) Well! That's that! I took that little mousie down a peg. Whew! His feet were like icicles. (*Turns to* LARRY.) Reminded me of when I was sleeping with you in that logger's cabin up in Canada, only your feet were bigger.

LARRY. Speaking of our trip, I thought it would be best if we told the girls what our surprise is.

REX. Possibly! If he landed here right out of the blue the shock might be too much for their little hearts to stand.

BILLIE. (*With interest*) He?

CONNIE. You mean you found the man you want up THERE?

(The boys look at each other and grin knowingly.)

LARRY. I think we might be so bold as to refer to it as a man, eh, Rex?

REX. Oh, sure, sure! Provided we slide over a few of the major points.

BILLIE. Well, go ahead and tell us.

CONNIE. Yes, do. We're just dying to hear. (*She and* BILLIE *sit on divan.*)

LARRY. One night about dark we ran onto a sort of cabin in no-man's land. It must have been over a hundred miles from the nearest town, wasn't it, Rex?

REX. A mere hundred? When my dogs were barking up the family tree the way they were? Brother Larry, it was a thousand miles we walked that day if we toddled an inch.

LARRY. It must have been around a hundred. We'd walked over two days.

REX. It was a hundred a day at least.

LARRY. Anyway, in this cabin was a young fellow.

BILLIE. Really! Was he good-looking?

REX. Good-looking? (*Dryly.*) Heh! Heh! Heh!

LARRY. He was a regulation hermit.

REX. (*Mysteriously*) Yeah man! And you should have seen one room in that little old cabin.

LARRY. I'll say! This geezer told us that his uncle had just died.

CONNIE. Oh, that's too bad. Was he all alone?

REX. Alone? That guy was so all alone he didn't even cast a shadow.

LARRY. It turned out that his uncle was a very clever

scientist who had been disappointed in love—we figured that out for ourselves—as this young guy was pretty innocent.

Rex. Yeah, that was our deduction of the situation.

Larry. The kid's father and mother were killed when he was just a lad and, before he could remember, his uncle dragged him off to that lonely cabin and he's been there ever since.

Billie. (*Breathlessly*) Oh! How adventurous!

Rex. Sure! Horatio Alger in real life.

Larry. This uncle seems to have been a confirmed woman hater.

Rex. We're sure we're right on that score because we never even found one picture of a woman in the cabin.

Connie. My goodness! How odd!

Rex. Odd? It was plain depressing.

Billie. (*Incredulously*) But what did they use for pin-ups?

Rex. (*Distastefully*) Pictures of bearded scientists.

Larry. The uncle made the only trips to civilization and the boy never went further than the river, about two miles below.

Billie. I'll bet the old boy had a girl friend at the trading post.

Larry. We know this is hard to believe but—(*pauses for emphasis*) not only has that boy never seen a woman but he doesn't have the faintest idea of what they are like. In fact he thinks they're some sort of a *pet* that men have.

Connie. (*Unbelievingly*) Not really?

Rex. It's the truth, so help me Hannah.

Larry. The uncle taught the boy all about science and, believe it or not, that's all the boy knows. (*Grins.*) He surely wonders what the rest of the world is like.

Rex. So we invited him down-river to visit us and to learn how the rest of the world lives.

Billie. (*Excitedly*) He's coming here? How wonderful!

Connie. When is he coming, Larry?

Larry. Tonight! I arranged for a plane to land him

at the airport and I have a taxi awaiting him there. He should be here anytime. Rex and I will meet him at the door and sneak him upstairs so we can make him presentable before we introduce him.

BILLIE. (*Excitedly*) Come on, Connie! We've got to get ready.

LARRY. Now you girls fix some lunch and Rex and I will see if we can get some clothes together.

BILLIE. Clothes? Doesn't he wear any?

REX. A bearskin!

LARRY. He said he had " dress-up " clothes but we never saw them. His uncle ordered them from a mail order catalog, so it isn't hard to imagine what they'll be.

CONNIE. Call us when he's presentable. Come on, Billie. We'd better hurry. (*Starts* L.)

BILLIE. (*Following her*) This is going to be fun! (*Giggles.*) The boys said he's never seen a woman. What do you suppose he'll think *we* are?   [*They exit* L.

REX. I sure don't want to miss the look on that geezer's map the first time he sees a woman.

LARRY. (*Who has started upstairs, pauses*) By the way, what in heck did he say his name was? (*Is leaning over the stair railing.*)

REX. Do you mean to stand there, I mean lean there, and tell me you've actually forgotten his handle?

LARRY. So help me, I can't recall it, yet it seems as though it was something I should never forget.

REX. I'll say you shouldn't! That guy's name is about as much like him as I am like a jackass.

LARRY. Then it must fit him like a glove.

REX. Yeah? You forgotten your Shakespeare?

LARRY. That's right! It was a Shakespearean name.

REX. I should hope to croak it was. His last name is Montague. Doesn't that tip bring anything to that void you call a mind?

LARRY. (*Thoughtfully*) Montague! Montague! (*Suddenly grins.*) Oh, my gosh! Romeo Montague! What a name for a hermit!

REX. Our little backwoods Romeo! Whee! Wait until we introduce him to the girls.

LARRY. They won't believe that name.

REX. Who would? Even we had to be convinced by his hunting and fishing license.

LARRY (*As he exits stairs*) I hope he brings them along for identification.

REX. (*Following* LARRY *off*) If he doesn't, we'll never be able to prove we aren't pulling a colossal gag.

(LA REINA *enters* L. *and goes to adjust divan which the furniture movers left slightly out of place. While she is working at it* BILLIE *enters* L.)

BILLIE. Here! I'll help you.

LA REINA. (*Pushing and grunting*) It is—how you say? Pesado?

BILLIE. (*Helping her*) You mean heavy?

LA REINA. Si! It is heavy. Gracias, Senorita. Thank you.

BILLIE. La Reina! We're expecting company any minute. Perhaps you'd better unlock the front door.

LA REINA. (*Glancing* R. *nervously*) But the termites, Senorita!

BILLIE. (*Finishing adjusting pillows*) Termites?

LA REINA. The muebles, the furniture movers, Senorita.

BILLIE. Oh! It's all right. We saw them drive away. They won't be back until tomorrow at least. Perhaps Larry can think of a good one by then.

LA REINA. Si! O. K.! Bueno! I unlock him!

[*Exits* R.

CONNIE. (*Appears in door* L. *as* LA REINA *exits* R.) Good for you, Billie. You're getting things straightened out.

BILLIE. La Reina and I managed. (*Thoughtfully.*) Connie! I wonder what this—this hermit is really like.

CONNIE. (*Dismissing the subject*) Oh, probably like a hermit—er—any hermit, that is.

BILLIE. But they spoke as though he is young. Do you suppose he would be at all good-looking?

CONNIE. Good heavens, no! They said he dresses in a bearskin and he probably has a beard.

BILLIE. Oh, I hope not. They tickle.

CONNIE. Who ever saw a hermit who didn't have a beard? (*Looks around room.*) Well, it looks normal again. I surely hope Larry can work out something so we won't have to lose all this.

BILLIE (*Hopefully*) Perhaps this hermit really has brains.

CONNIE. Let's hope he has. He probably hasn't anything else.

BILLIE. (*Dropping into armchair*) It'll be an experience—meeting him, I mean.

CONNIE. (*Distastefully*) No doubt! (*Starts* L. *but turns at door.*) There's one thing we'll have to be careful of, Billie.

BILLIE. Something about the hermit?

CONNIE. We'll have to be poker-faced. It would be embarrassing to all of us if we should laugh when we're introduced to him.

LA REINA. (*Enters* R.) Miss Connie! There is a Senor Montague waiting outside.

CONNIE. Montague?

BILLIE. We don't know anyone by that name. (*Excitedly.*) Connie! I'll bet it's the hermit.

CONNIE. I wonder. What does he look like, La Reina?

LA REINA. (*Soulfully*) Oh, Senorita! Beautiful, Senorita, *beautiful!*

BILLIE. No! It's not the hermit.

CONNIE. If it's not him I can't imagine who in the world it can be. Show him in, La Reina. (*Starts out* L.)

BILLIE. Aren't you going to stay, Connie?

[LA REINA *exits* R.

CONNIE. No, you can attend to him, whoever he is.

BILLIE. But I don't know the guy.

CONNIE. Neither do I. It's probably someone who wants to see Larry or Rex, or both. You can make him comfortable until they appear.   [*Exits* L.

BILLIE. (*Grumbling to herself as she crosses to divan*)

Shucks! I always have to receive the uninteresting characters around this dump.

LA REINA. (*Enters* R., *pausing just inside door to
make her announcement*) Mr. Montague, Miss Billie!
(*Walks to door* L. *where she turns and sighs, eyes on
door* R., *then exits.*)

(ROMEO MONTAGUE *enters slowly and wonderingly
door* R. *We find him to be the direct opposite of
what one might expect of any self-respecting hermit.
Movies, novels and plays to the contrary,* ROMEO *is
very much up-to-date in his physical appearance—in
fact, he is attired in the height of fashion. The time
being late afternoon he has come to spend the evening
and is dressed in a neat up-to-the-minute tuxedo and
his athletic figure lends to his appearance a touch of
having stepped forth from the latest fashion plate.
He is neatly combed and deeply tanned. He stops
just inside door and* BILLIE *turns to face him, looks
away, and then helps herself to a generous double-
take. Her mouth drops open and she stares at him
in anything but a ladylike manner.*)

BILLIE. (*Stuttering*) Oh! Me excuse! I mean excuse me! Good evening! How do you do! How are
you! I'm awfully pleased to—to —— I haven't met you
before, have I?

ROMEO. (*Speaking precisely and with rather a near
Oxford accent*) No, I cannot recall our having met before.

BILLIE. That being the case I—I—er—I'm pleased to
meet you.

ROMEO. (*With a slight bow, his eyes intent on* BILLIE)
Thank you!

BILLIE. Er—my name's Billie.

ROMEO. (*Gravely*) I'm delighted to make your ac-
quaintance, Billie.

BILLIE. (*Almost trills*) Ohhh! Thank you! And
who are you?

ROMEO. (*Matter-of-factly*) I am Romeo!

BILLIE.   And I am delighted to —— (*She stops and gasps.*)   What—er—who did you say you were?

ROMEO.   I beg your pardon for not explaining.   Romeo is my cognomen.   (BILLIE *stares blankly at him, shaking her head.*)   My appellation!   (*She still stares unbelievingly.*)   In short, my name is Romeo.

BILLIE.   (*To herself*)   Too short if you ask me.   Exactly what did you say that name of yours was?

ROMEO.   (*A trifle impatiently*)   I stated quite positively that my name is Romeo.

BILLIE.   (*Hesitatingly*)   That—that's what I thought you said.   (*Indicating armchair.*)   Won't you have a seat?

ROMEO.   Thank you!   (*He sits, sinks down in the soft chair and jumps up alarmed and stands looking at chair.*)

BILLIE.   It's all right.   You won't go through.   (ROMEO *gingerly feels chair then slowly and cautiously lowers himself into it.*)   You're a stranger around here, aren't you?

ROMEO.   I am indeed.

BILLIE.   Do you plan to live here?

ROMEO.   Oh, no!   Not at all.   I am here in answer to an invitation.   Lawrence McNeil resides here, does he not?

BILLIE.   Yes, he does.   Are you a friend of Larry's?

ROMEO.   Most assuredly, but don't disturb him if he is occupied.

BILLIE.   He won't mind being interrupted.   He and Rex Simonds are getting ready for some queer outlandish duck they have coming to see us.

ROMEO.   (*Puzzled*)   Duck?

BILLIE.   (*With an airy gesture*)   You know—some goofy geezer they picked up.

ROMEO.   (*Definitely puzzled*)   "Goofy geezer?"

BILLIE.   (*Smiling*)   Don't let it worry you.   They asked him to drop in and visit them.   He's just some old backwoods bromide.

ROMEO.   (*Thoughtfully*)   "Backwoods bromide!"

BILLIE.   Larry and Rex took a long trek away up into the hinterlands and ran across a hermit of all things. (*She laughs as though the idea was absolutely ridiculous*

but Romeo, *who is catching on as to whom she is referring, does not share her humor.*)

Romeo.   I see! A hermit.

Billie.   Yes, but let's not talk about him. He's just a
lonesome timberwolf with a long beard who wears a
bearskin. We needn't discuss him.

Romeo.   (*Carefully*) Please *do* discuss him. I somehow feel a kinship with him. You say he has a beard?

Billie.   The boys didn't actually *say* he has a beard
but of course he has. You know how hermits are.

Romeo.   No, I know very little about them.

Billie.   Haven't you ever seen a hermit? A real
honest-to-goodness one, I mean?

Romeo.   N-n-no, as a matter of fact I have never met
one.

Billie.   Well! Where've you been all your life?

Romeo.   (*Hesitatingly*) I—I hope you will pardon
me for declining to answer that question for the moment.

Billie.   Oh, that's all right. You're more fascinating
when I don't know anything about you.

Romeo.   Fascinating? (*Incredulously.*) Do you mean
to infer that *I* fascinate you?

Billie.   (*Matter-of-factly*) Of course! Any strange
handsome man always fascinates me.

Romeo.   I—I never met anyone exactly like you before.

Billie.   Oh, that's just your line. (*Giggles.*) But I
like it.

Romeo.   My—er—" line " did you say?

Billie.   Sure. I know you're just stringing me.

Romeo.   " Stringing!" (*Slowly.*) I do not believe
that I understand your meaning. I am conversant with
the culinary art of stringing beans but how does one go
about the process of " stringing " a human being?

Billie.   (*Astonished*) Do you mean that you don't
know? Honestly?

Romeo.   (*Smiling*) I am afraid I do not.

Billie.   (*Attempts to explain*) Well, you throw them
a line—er—just sorta string them along. (*Hopefully.*)
Get it?

ROMEO. Do I " get it "? If by that you mean do I understand, most assuredly I do not.

BILLIE. (*Taking another tack*) Well, you've heard of pulling the wool over one's eyes, haven't you?

ROMEO. " Pulling the wool." I've heard of wool being taken from sheep but —— (*Very much dazed.*) No!

BILLIE. (*Getting a bit rattled*) You've heard of bulldozing, of course?

ROMEO. Oh, most assuredly. I saw ——

BILLIE. There you are. Bulldozing! Pulling the wool over your eyes! Stringing! Throwing a line—they're all the same.

ROMEO. But bulldozing is accomplished by means of a gigantic vehicle. I saw such a machine at a mine where I visited.

CONNIE. (*Enters* L. *wearing apron*) Billie! Will you —— Oh, I beg your pardon. I forgot you had company.

BILLIE. Meet Larry's friend, Connie. He SAYS his name is Romeo.

CONNIE. How do you do!

BILLIE. This is my sister, Connie McNeil.

ROMEO. (*Gravely*) How do you do, Mr. McNeil?

CONNIE. Mister?

ROMEO. (*To himself*) Sister!

CONNIE. I beg your pardon.

ROMEO. I am sorry. I was communing with myself. A pernicious habit I must confess.

CONNIE. Have you called Larry, Billie?

BILLIE. No! Mr. Romeo and I have been having a fascinating conversation. I'll call him now.

CONNIE. Please do, right away. I need your help in getting ready for the boys' backwoods yokel friend.

ROMEO. (*To himself*) " Backwoods yokel."

BILLIE. (*Looks at* ROMEO *a bit disgustedly then goes to stairs and calls*) Larreeee! You have company.

CONNIE. I'm very glad to have met you, Mr. ——

ROMEO. Montague. Romeo Montague.

CONNIE. (*A bit nettled*) Who do you think you —— Oh, never mind. I hope you'll excuse me. Come, Billie!

ROMEO. Certainly.

BILLIE. (*Crossing to* CONNIE *at door* L.) Larry'll be right down.

ROMEO. (*Rising for the first time*) I hope you'll excuse a seeming morbid curiosity on my part but you have an odd voice.

BILLIE. (*Indignantly*) Oh, I have, have I?

ROMEO. Yes, both of you have.

CONNIE. Well! I like that.

BILLIE. (*Challengingly*) What's wrong with our voices?

ROMEO. I *presume* they are all right. In fact, I like them. They are rather soothing to the auditory senses.

CONNIE. Oh, for —— Come on, Billie! [*She exits* L.

BILLIE. (*Giggling*) Be seeing you!

CONNIE. (*Reaches through door and jerks* BILLIE *off*) I said come on!

ROMEO. (*Looks after them puzzled*) They're the oddest *men* I have ever known. (*Paces back and forth talking to himself.*) It is evident they lack manliness but— I rather like them. (*He turns and gazes at door* L.)

LARRY. (*Appears on stair landing. He stops and looks questioningly at* ROMEO, *then his face lights with recognition*) Romeo! (*Runs downstairs and grabs* ROMEO'S *hand.*) Well, I'll be doggoned! (*Yells.*) Rex! It's Romeo! You sure look different than when we met you in the woods. At first I didn't know you.

ROMEO. I must confess that I feel differently.

LARRY. (*Pumping* ROMEO'S *hand*) I'm sure glad to see you.

ROMEO. I hope I don't appear too strange in these clothes. They are somewhat different from my accustomed attire.

REX. (*At head of stairs*) Romeo! (*Runs down and takes* ROMEO'S *hand.*) Holy mackerel! How'd you ever know him, Larry? Is he a changed chicken! Boy, you sure live up to your name now! (*Looks admiringly over* ROMEO.) Larry! He looks like ——. (*Mentions the name of some popular male movie star.*)

ROMEO. It was with a great deal of difficulty that I

decided on the type of apparel in which to appear. My clothes all seemed so conservative. It did not seem apropos to attire myself in full evening dress.

Rex. Don't tell us you were contemplating full soup and fish?

Romeo. Oh, no. I am not at all hungry.

Larry. (*Laughing*) Don't let Rex kid you. "Soup and fish" is just slang for full evening dress.

Romeo. Slang?

Rex. Don't you even know what slang is?

Romeo. I must confess that I do not.

(Larry *and* Rex *exchange glances.*)

Rex. Er—you know about conjugation, or do you?

Romeo. Most assuredly. Is that slang?

Rex. Er—not exactly. We say, sling, slang, slung. Today we'll sling it. Yesterday we slung it and tomorrow we'll slang it. Slang is a sort of future language, just a few years ahead of the dictionary. (Romeo *shakes his head discouraged.* Rex *looks at* Larry *and tries again.*) It's this way: We SLANG a word for awhile and that gets people to SLINGING it and finally it gets SLUNG into the dictionary. Sling, slang, slung! Get it?

Romeo. My erudition must be deficient for I find that I am not at all conversant with the anomalous colloquialisms with which you have imbued your vocabulary. I fear I must concede myself to be irretrievably nescious.

Rex. (*Staring stupidly at* Romeo) Will you kindly remove your tonsils and indulge in a bit of reiteration?

Romeo. My tonsils were removed when I was a mere child—so I've been told.

Rex. (*A bit angry*) Say! Are you trying to pull my leg?

Romeo. (*Indignantly*) Of course not! I have not touched you.

Rex. (*Helplessly to* Larry) I throw in the sponge!

Romeo. (*Contritely*) I am so sorry. Did I interrupt your bath?

Rex. (*Wearily*) No, you didn't, but I can see where

I've gotta get into a huddle with Noah Webster if this keeps up. (*To* Larry.) WE'VE got to learn to speak English.

Romeo. (*Thoughtfully*) I have been advised that Noah Webster died.

Rex. He did but thank heaven, he left his work for posterity and I'm part of Noah Webster's posterity.

Larry. (*Smiling*) This is no way to make Romeo feel at home. After your trip you probably want to clean up a bit. Later I'll introduce you to the rest of the McNeil household.

Romeo. (*Brightens*) Before you came down I chanced to meet two of your brothers.

Larry. MY brothers? But I haven't any brothers. (*To* Rex.) Or have I?

Romeo. You have no brothers? They referred to themselves as having the name of McNeil.

Rex. (*Watching* Larry *closely*) Just what did these McNeil brothers look like?

Romeo. I must admit I have never seen any MEN like them before today. Their clothing too was odd. I don't know what one would call it but only one wore trousers. But perhaps the other one wore a new type of dressing gown with which I am unfamiliar.

Rex. (*Winking at* Larry) Did they talk like this? (*In high falsetto.*) How do you do, Mr. Montague?

Romeo. (*Seriously*) Not exactly, although their voices were of a very light timbre. They had a much more soothing tone than the one you just assumed.

Rex. So you've already met Connie and Billie.

Romeo. That was the names they used, Connie and Billie. (*Interestedly.*) Is there something wrong with those men?

Larry. (*Trying hard to repress a laugh*) Well, as MEN there's something decidedly wrong.

Rex. So you never met any fellows like them?

Romeo. No, never.

Rex. Brother Romeo, you can thank your lucky stars you never did meet a man like that.

ROMEO. Really, you know, they seemed to fascinate me.

REX. (*Dryly*) You and a half dozen other guys.

ROMEO. Are they something different?

REX. *Very* different. And you'll find that YOU'LL be different once you get to know one of them well.

LARRY. (*Coming to* REX'S *rescue—he hopes*) Yes, they are—er—quite different, Romeo.

ROMEO. (*Incredulously*) Do you mean to say there are two entirely different types of men in the world?

REX. Well—er—I —— You tell him, Larry. I haven't the heart.

LARRY. (*Glaring at* REX) You're doing O. K. Well, there are men like you, Romeo, Rex and myself and —— (*Stops as he is stumped.*)

REX. (*Cutting in brightly*) Then there are men like Connie and Billie.

ROMEO. I must remember that. (*Starts with a new thought.*) Oh, by the way, are there any women here?

LARRY and REX. (*In unison*) Huh?

REX. What in the name of the great horned spoon do you think we were talking about?

ROMEO. But ——

LARRY. Just what did you ask, Romeo?

ROMEO. (*Patiently*) I asked if you have any women. You mentioned them up at the cabin.

REX. Women! Yeah, we have some women.

ROMEO. (*Delighted*) May I see one?

REX. (*Almost passing out*) Uh—you—ulp—sure! Sure he can see one, can't he, Larry?

LARRY. Didn't your uncle tell you *anything* about women?

ROMEO. Oh, my, yes. He told me ALL about them.

REX. ALL about them? He must have been a **wise** old guy.

LARRY. What did he tell you, Romeo?

ROMEO. Well, he explained they were some kind of a dumb animal and —— (*Pauses as he notices the look on faces of* REX *and* LARRY.) Is there something amiss?

REX. (*Gasping for breath*) Did—did you tell Billie and Connie that?

ROMEO. N-n-no, I can't recall that I did.

LARRY. What else did your uncle tell you about women?

ROMEO. He said some men were insane enough to take such people right into their homes and —— (LARRY *and* REX *nearly choke on this.*) What is the matter?

LARRY. Actually, you know *nothing* of women, do you?

ROMEO. Not first-hand information, of course, but Uncle Benvolio said the best possible place for them was in pens in the back yard. (*The boys laugh and* ROMEO *goes on apologetically.*) Of course, I've never even seen one of them.

REX. That's what *you* think, brother.

LARRY. Haven't you read about them?

ROMEO. (*Thoughtfully*) I presume some of the portions that Uncle Benvolio deleted from my reading matter may have been devoted to such morbid subjects.

REX. Well! All I can say is that you sure didn't have much to read if Uncle Bennie deleted everything that's written about women.

LARRY. (*Hopelessly to* REX) I'm afraid we have a problem child on our hands.

REX. (*Apprehensively*) I sure dread to have him wake up.

ROMEO. (*Disappointed*) I was hoping that you might enlighten me on the subject. My uncle was so reticent about women that I have become truly curious.

REX. Don't kid yourself, brother. Your Uncle Bennie's reticence didn't cause all the curiosity you feel boiling within you.

LARRY. Don't you remember your *mother?*

REX. Uncle Bennie told you about her, didn't he?

ROMEO. No, and I've often wondered about the origin ——

REX. Don't wonder any more. It's a ticklish subject. (*Turns to* LARRY.) What in the world can we tell the guy?

ROMEO. Do you mean to infer that there is something I don't *know?*

REX. (*Pityingly, as he places hand on* ROMEO'S *shoulder*) What you don't know is now packing to the doors every library and bookstore in the United States.

ROMEO. Do you mean to tell me there are things about women Uncle Benvolio did not tell me?

LARRY. W-e-l-l, he evidently omitted a *few* facts.

ROMEO. I see. From your remarks I would gather that women are considered of some significance.

REX. Well, that depends on whether you're talking to a woman or to a man.

ROMEO. (*Amazed*) Ohhhh! Do they—do they actually *talk?*

REX. (*Winking at* LARRY) If he only knew what's in store for him!

ROMEO. I presume their powers of speech somewhat resemble that of a parrot.

REX. You've got something there.

ROMEO. Then I suppose women have rather a large vocabulary?

REX. Uh-huh! That's putting it mildly.

ROMEO. How interesting! Then they must be among the intelligent forms of animal life.

(*This is again too much for* LARRY *and* REX.)

REX. I wouldn't miss the next few hours for all the money in the world.

ROMEO. (*Puzzled and slightly hurt*) I have not attempted to be humorous. Why do my remarks provoke so much levity?

REX. (*Taking* ROMEO'S *arm*) Forget it. Come upstairs where you can wash up and take an opiate —— You'll need it—considering what's ahead!

ROMEO. I have never felt more serene in my life. My journey down here was highly entertaining.

LARRY. (*Dryly*) We weren't referring to your journey down here.

REX. Oh, no! Nothing as easy as that. It's your

proposed journey into the feminine dimension to which WE refer.

(*They start leading him up the stairway.*)

Romeo. " Feminine dimension? " I don't understand. " Feminine ——"

Rex. Oh, come on. Now I've seen and heard everything.

(*They force* Romeo *upstairs, both laughing,* Romeo *looking from one to the other in utter bewilderment. The three boys barely disappear before doorbell is heard off* R. La Reina *enters* L., *crosses, and exits* R. Billie *enters* L., *goes back of divan, and stands watching door* R. La Reina *enters* R., *followed by* Orpha Finley, *an attractive, reserved girl in her early twenties. She wears a modish coat, gown and hat and carries purse and gloves.*)

La Reina. (*Speaking as she enters*) The Senor Larry is upstairs.

Billie. Hi, Orpha!

Orpha. Hello! Don't bother to call him, La Reina. I'll have a chat with Billie and Connie first.

La Reina. Si, Senorita.   [*Exits* L.

Orpha. (*Sitting* R. C.) What's new, Billie?

Billie. Plenty! (*Sits on divan.*) I really *have* something to tell you today.

Orpha. Sounds interesting. We need something interesting in this one-horse summer resort.

Billie. You know how mysterious Larry and Rex were when they returned from their Canadian trip?

Orpha. They about devastated our collective feminine curiosity. Have they decided to divulge the deep, dark secret?

Connie. (*Enters* L.) Hello, Orpha! I thought I heard your voice.

Billie. I'm just starting to tell Orpha the big news.

Orpha. Better hurry or you'll have a nervous wreck before you.

BILLIE. Well, Larry and Rex got way up in Canada—
a hundred miles from nowhere—and they found a hermit
in a cabin.

ORPHA. (*Shrugs*) Well? Every self-respecting hermit lives by himself in a cabin a hundred miles from nowhere.

CONNIE. (*Sitting beside* BILLIE) Wait until you hear
all of it.

BILLIE. Yes, just wait. The boys said he was young,
had a long beard, dressed in a bearskin, and you could
smell ——

CONNIE. Billie! You're using your imagination.

BILLIE. Suppose I am? They didn't have to describe
him. We all know what a hermit looks like.

ORPHA. What's this hermit got to do with us?

BILLIE. They've invited him here.

ORPHA. (*Instantly interested*) They have? When's
he due to arrive?

BILLIE. Any minute. Isn't it exciting?

CONNIE. I suppose he's on his way down the big river
in a canoe.

BILLIE. Isn't that the most excitingly *exciting* news
you've ever heard? And isn't it the most unusual *unusual*
news you ever heard, too?

ORPHA. I'll admit it has the makings of an interesting
experience.

BILLIE. He's a scientist and Larry thinks he may get
some scientific discovery out of him. Then he can claim
his inheritance.

ORPHA. From a hermit? If I were Larry I wouldn't
bank on that too much.

BILLIE. I wonder who that awfully handsome fellow
was who stopped in to see Larry?

CONNIE. Someone Larry met recently, I suppose. He's
always bringing some strange character home or inviting
him to call.

BILLIE. That boy's no character. He was dressed in
a brand new tux and he sure looked handsome to me,
honey.

ORPHA. You shouldn't be interested in handsome strangers, Billie. You're going steady with Rex.

BILLIE. What of it? Does going steady with Rex revoke my hunting license?

CONNIE. Whoever Pretty Boy was he's some wag. I wonder who he thinks he is? Huh! He had the nerve to introduce himself as Romeo.

BILLIE. He's handsome enough to be Romeo, isn't he?

CONNIE. Just because he's a bit good-looking you'd forgive him anything.

ORPHA. Don't tell him, of course, but I'm perfectly satisfied with Larry's good looks. Besides, looks aren't everything.

BILLIE. Perhaps not but they're sure easy on the eyes. If I had a face like Romeo's to gaze on for the rest of my life I'd never need glasses.

CONNIE. Well, we won't have to worry about the hermit's good looks for he won't have any.

BILLIE. I suppose not but I sure hope he has something, if it's only a mysterious gleam in his eyes.

CONNIE. (*Rising*) Come on, Orpha, help us with the lunch. You'll have plenty of time to spoon with Larry later.

ORPHA. (*Also rising*) How do you know that Larry and I have reached the spooning point?

BILLIE. Perhaps it's just the scrapping point. Larry says you're practically engaged.

ORPHA. (*As she follows* BILLIE *and* CONNIE L.) Oh, he does? How nice of big brother to tell everyone but me.

BILLIE. (*As she exits* L.) He just mentioned it. Please don't tell him I said anything.

ORPHA. Your big brother and I are going to have a little talk and pronto. [*She and* CONNIE *exit* L.

(LARRY *appears at head of stairs. He looks around, sees no one, motions off stairs, and* ROMEO *appears behind him.*)

LARRY. (*As they descend stairs*) I thought I heard the girls.

ROMEO. (*Puzzled*) Girls?
LARRY. Don't you even know what girls are?
ROMEO. Should I?
LARRY. No! I'm expecting too much. Suppose you make yourself at home here. I've something to say to Rex.
ROMEO. Don't bother about me. Please do not allow my presence to demoralize your usual agenda.
LARRY. (*Looks at* ROMEO *a moment without speaking*) I'm glad someone thinks I have an agenda. I didn't realize my life was that orderly. Now just make yourself comfortable. I'll be down in a jiffy. (*Starts for stairs.*)
ROMEO. Jiffy?
LARRY. Forgot again! I should say, in a *minute*.
                              [*Exits stairs.*
ROMEO. (*Looks at* LARRY) " Jiffy? " Hum! " Minute? " (*Sighs.*) It's all so odd.
CONNIE. (*Appears in door* L.) Larry! I—— Oh, I beg your pardon, Mr. Montague. I thought Larry was here.
ROMEO. He was but returned above to commune with Rex. I told him to proceed with his usual agenda.
CONNIE. (*Curiously*) You're not a local boy, are you? (*Stands back of divan.*)
ROMEO. (*Puzzled*) " Local boy? " Oh, you mean I am not a permanent resident of your city? No, I am not.
CONNIE. Mind telling me where you're from?
ROMEO. Not at all. I am from across the river in Canada.
CONNIE. How interesting. When did you move here?
ROMEO. I have not moved. I merely made the journey to visit with Larry and Rex.
CONNIE. I've never heard them mention you. When did you arrive?
ROMEO. A few minutes before I came here. I've never seen a town this size before. It is all very fascinating to me.
CONNIE. (*Smiling*) I suppose it does seem rather small after Toronto and Montreal.

Romeo. I have never seen Toronto or Montreal. I am from a very small community.

Connie. Then what makes this town fascinate you? Is it so much smaller than towns you've been in?

Romeo. Oh, no! It is a great deal larger.

Connie. (*Surprised*) Larger?

Romeo. Yes indeed! But I am afraid I am interrupting your preparations for this—this visitor you are expecting.

Connie. Oh, Billie and Orpha can attend to him. Besides, he's just a hermit Rex and Larry picked up.

Romeo. (*Carefully*) Have you seen this—hermit?

Connie. (*Indifferently*) Oh, no! You know how such people are. They have long beards and wear animal skins.

Romeo. Oh, they do?

Connie. Oh, my goodness, yes.

Romeo. Somehow I feel there is something strangely amiss.

Connie. I thought everyone knew what hermits looked like.

Romeo. (*Cautiously*) I have never given them a great deal of thought.

Connie. Haven't you seen them in the movies?

Romeo. " Movies? "

Connie. I mean in the motion pictures.

Romeo. " Motion pictures! " Mmmmmm!

Connie. Perhaps you refer to them as the cinema as they do in England.

Romeo. (*Apologetically*) I am frightfully sorry but I seem to be completely at a loss as to what you are talking about.

Connie. (*Looks puzzled but continues*) Perhaps you refer to them as legitimate drama then?

Romeo. Oh! You are referring to drama. Of course I have read dramas. I believe I like Shakespeare best, though Ibsen, Moliere and their contemporaries ——

Connie. I love Shakespeare, too, although he always kept his women's parts rather small.

ROMEO.   Women's parts?   Are women depicted in Shakespeare's plays?

CONNIE.   Of course! You know of Portia, Lady Macbeth, Desdemona ——

ROMEO.   Were *they* women?

CONNIE.   (*Dryly*) That's what the scripts tell us.

ROMEO.   (*Bewildered*) How odd!

CONNIE.   What's so odd about it?

ROMEO.   (*Uncertainly*) Of course Uncle Benvolio edited everything I read ——

CONNIE.   Your uncle, did you say?

ROMEO.   Yes. Uncle Benvolio reared me from a mere child.

CONNIE.   (*A bit enlightened*) Oh, he did?

ROMEO.   Of course. That is how it happens I have a cognomen of Shakespearean derivation. Uncle Benvolio was named for the Shakespearean character and was also responsible for the appellation which is now attached to me.

CONNIE.   (*Half to herself*) "Romeo Montague!" I should have guessed it immediately.

ROMEO.   May I inquire what you should have guessed?

CONNIE.   You're the young man Larry and Rex found in the cabin a hundred miles from nowhere.

ROMEO.   I am afraid you have been misinformed.

CONNIE.   Have I?

ROMEO.   Yes! The settlement of Nowhere is just across the lake from my cabin.

CONNIE.   (*Trying to keep from laughing*) Really?

ROMEO.   (*Earnestly*) Yes! My cabin is a hundred miles from the Trading Post, not a hundred miles from Nowhere. Now do you understand?

CONNIE.   (*With a half giggle*) And what's the name of the Trading Post?

ROMEO.   Where-Are-We.

CONNIE.   I asked the name of the Trading ——

ROMEO.   This-Is-It.

CONNIE.   What is it?

ROMEO.   Where-Are-We.

CONNIE. (*Exasperated*) We're at the name of the Trading Post and ——

ROMEO. I fear you misapprehend. Where-Are-We ——

CONNIE. (*Quickly*) I'm trying to tell you where we are.

ROMEO. The name of the Trading Post is Where-Are-We. Where-Are-We is a hundred miles from Nowhere.

CONNIE. And just where do you live?

ROMEO. I told you, just directly across the lake from Nowhere.

CONNIE. What's the name of your cabin?

ROMEO. This-Is-It.

CONNIE. (*After a slight pause*) Well?

ROMEO. This-Is-It.

CONNIE. WHAT is it?

ROMEO. THIS-IS-IT.

CONNIE. I don't get it.

ROMEO. Do you mean that you do not understand?

CONNIE. That's precisely what I mean.

ROMEO. This-Is-It is the name of my cabin.

CONNIE. (*Enlightened*) Oh, I see now! By saying THAT is it, you mean THIS is it and This-Is-It is the name of your cabin which is situated on a lake a hundred miles from Where-Are-We and Where-Are-We is a hundred miles from Nowhere which is located directly across the lake from This-Is-It. My! How simple!

ROMEO. (*All smiles*) Isn't it?

CONNIE. I should have tumbled immediately. By the way, I understand you're something of a scientist.

ROMEO. I prefer to refer to myself as a student of science. My personal scientific achievements are still in the elementary stage.

CONNIE. Now you're just being modest.

ROMEO. Not at all. Actually, I was still serving my apprenticeship when my Uncle Benvolio passed away.

CONNIE. What kind of scientific experiments did your uncle perform?

ROMEO. His major interest lay in atomic research.

CONNIE. (*Skeptically*) Really? Of course you've

heard of atomic bombs which were dropped in World War II?

ROMEO. Yes, but what was used then was made obsolete by developments brought about by Uncle Benvolio.

CONNIE. (*Amazed*) You mean to imply that your dear departed uncle split atoms before the greatest scientists in the world could manage that little trick?

ROMEO. You have introduced a technical point. THEY split atoms while my uncle caused them to explode.

CONNIE. (*Suddenly laughing*) You're kidding.

ROMEO. "Kidding?"

CONNIE. I mean joking.

ROMEO. Not at all. I am being very serious.

CONNIE. I think you've lived alone so long you're imagining things.

ROMEO. (*Seriously*) No, it's the truth. I swear it.

CONNIE. (*Laughs lightly as she turns away*) I can see that you're not accustomed to being with women.

ROMEO. (*Stares incredulously*) What did you say?

CONNIE. I merely said it's obvious you're not accustomed to being with women.

ROMEO. Women? WHEN have I been in the presence of a *woman?*

CONNIE. Oh, for heaven's sake! Don't try that line on me.

ROMEO. "Line?"

CONNIE. Don't stand there and try to tell me that you don't know Billie and I are women.

ROMEO. (*Almost strangling*) You—ulp—and bub—ulp—B-Billie—*women?* But—but women are *animals.*

CONNIE. (*Indignantly*) Oh, they are, are they? Who told you that?

ROMEO. (*Stammering and gulping*) Unc-Uncle Benvolio. He—he—said—that—that—women were—er—a sort of—er—pet that some men were low enough to l-l-let live in a house. He—he said it was like keeping chickens in the house. Unc-Uncle Benvolio said that women should be kept in a coop.

CONNIE. (*Angrily*) Is that so! Well, I'm a woman

and just try keeping me in a coop. (*To herself.*) Unless it has four wheels and a motor.

ROMEO. (*Wiping his forehead with handkerchief*) This—this is amazing. Then—then women are female men?

CONNIE. Oh, don't be such a sap! Don't you know your mother was a woman?

ROMEO. Did you know my mother? I mean wasn't she—he—a man?

CONNIE. Well, hardly. She was a WOMAN.

ROMEO. (*Breathlessly*) Ohhhh! (*He sways a moment then slowly sinks to floor in a dead faint.*)

CONNIE. (*Screaming*) LARRY! REX! BILLIE! ORPHA! COME HERE, QUICK!

(*There is a bedlam of voices off stage. LARRY and REX enter stairs. BILLIE and ORPHA both get to door L. at same time and struggle to get through, all talking at once.*)

ALL. It's Romie! What happened? Is he dead? Passed out! Did you hit him, Connie? Lift his feet! Drop his head! Get water!

(*LARRY and REX pick ROMEO up and put him on divan.*)

LARRY. Now what happened, Connie?

CONNIE. (*Hysterically*) I just told him that Billie and I are women.

REX. Oh! Now we know what's wrong with the guy. He's fainted.

CONNIE. Billie! Get a wet towel.

BILLIE. Why would a good-looking guy like him want to faint? With a face and figure like he's got he must have had plenty of women around him. (*Starts for door L.*)

LARRY. (*Who is working over ROMEO*) Get a pillow for his head!

(*CONNIE hands pillow to LARRY.*)

BILLIE. (*At door* L.) Who in heck *is* he, Larry?

CONNIE. He's the hermit, you ninny!

BILLIE. (*Screeches*) Eeeeeeek! Ohhhhh! (*She drops to floor in faint.*)

REX. Now *she's* fainted! (*Runs to* BILLIE.)

CONNIE. Orpha! Get TWO wet towels. (*Sways and sinks to floor as* ORPHA *dashes out* L.)

LARRY. Holy cats! Three of 'em passed out.

ORPHA. (*Dashes in* L. *with wet towel*) Here! I—I—— (*Starts to sway.*) The hermit!

LARRY. O. K.! Go ahead and faint! (ORPHA *does so.*) I'll get *four* wet towels! (*Dashes out* L. *leaving* REX *undecided as to which girl to help.*)

QUICK CURTAIN

ACT II

*(Stage is empty when curtain rises. Doorbell is heard
ringing off R. LA REINA hurries downstairs hum-
ming, goes to door R. and starts out only to bump
squarely into FOREWOMAN of the furniture company.)*

FOREWOMAN. *(Exasperated)* YOU again! Do we
have to start in where we left off last night?

LA REINA. *(Backing toward divan as FOREWOMAN
advances into room)* YOU—you old no-look-where-you-
goer!

FOREWOMAN. Never mind the double talk and don't
bother to call your boss. This is my last call for the day
on my road home and I've come for the fixin's and mouse
or no mouse, we're a-gonna take 'em this time.

LA REINA. *(Runs to foot of stairs and yells)* Senor!
Senorita! Mister Larry! These termites again!
(Catches herself and goes back to face the FOREWOMAN.)
No! He is in—in—Liberia! Biblioteca! Los ——

FOREWOMAN. *(Advancing to LA REINA)* None of
that stuff! I'm tellin' you —— *(She is literally standing
on LA REINA'S feet.)*

LA REINA. *(Thoroughly angry, shoves FOREWOMAN
back)* Ohhhh! Will you so please to look where I am
go and then will you so please to take yourself to some
place that is else? *(Rushes angrily to door L. and exits.)*

FOREWOMAN. *(Glaring after LA REINA)* Go myself
to some place that is else? I wish I wasn't dressed up like
a man. I'd show her what's what around here. *(Turns
and faces door R.)* Come and get it! *(The helpers, all
four of them, enter R. and move lackadaisically toward
divan.)* Step on it a bit! Take the same stuff that we
started with last night but TAKE it this time. If you see

a mouse, just stand still (*at word mouse all four helpers stand stock still*) while *I* call a cat. (*Glares at door* L.) That one that just left oughta do. Now MOVE!

(*The helpers slowly start to surround the divan as* LARRY *enters* L. *followed by* LA REINA. *The helpers look toward* LARRY, *shrug their shoulders in unison and all sit on divan, hands folded in lap.*)

LARRY. That's right, girls, don't let it get away.
FOREWOMAN. (*Sarcastically*) Well, big, beautiful and broke! What's your tale o' woe this time?
LARRY. THIS time I have some real news for you.
FOREWOMAN, Oh, yeah?
LA REINA. (*Nodding vigorously*) Si! Si!
FOREWOMAN. See what?
LA REINA. Si! Si! Yes!
FOREWOMAN. (*Looking around*) I don't see any-thing.
LARRY. " Si " is Spanish for yes.
REX. (*Appears on stairs,* BILLIE *right behind him*) Hey, Larry! I've just been talking to Romeo and I don't believe that he —— Oh! Oh! (*Goes downstairs.*) I see the demotivated penguins are back on our couch.
BILLIE. (*Descending stairs*) What do you mean " our couch "? You aren't a member of the family.
REX. I will be, chicken, if you but say the word.

(LA REINA *shrugs her shoulders and exits* L.)

FOREWOMAN. (*Irritably*) Do I have to stand here and listen to a couple of moon-eyed puppies gargle woo? Do I?
REX. Not at all. (*Points* R.) There's the door for you and your crew and don't forget your coveralls.
FOREWOMAN. (*Contemptuously*) Huh! (*Turns to* LARRY.) O. K.! O. K.! Is what you've got to say worth the use of my ears? Go ahead and be sure to make it big enough to fill 'em.
REX. Oh, my gosh! Has it got to be THAT big?

FOREWOMAN. Listen, you little sawed-off tub with legs on it! I usta be a strong woman in a circus. (*Advances meaningly toward him.*)

REX. (*Backing away from her*) And I used to be a sprinter in a college.

BILLIE. Fraidy-cat! Always sprinting away from trouble.

REX. Just like a woman. Because I've never found anything worth fighting for she thinks I'm a coward.

LARRY. You two kids have the craziest way of sparking.

BILLIE. (*Resentfully*) I'll have you understand we're *not* sparking!

REX. That's right. I sure wish you'd work on a little de-icing.

LARRY. Whatever you're doing, will you please forget it for now? (*Turns toward* FOREWOMAN.) I have some business to transact with this LADY.

FOREWOMAN. Now I *know* you're going to pull a fast one. No man ever called me a lady unless he wanted to borrow some money or sell me something.

LARRY. You shouldn't be so suspicious.

FOREWOMAN. O. K.! Suppose you turn on your de-suspicioner and give me one good reason, *just one,* as to why I should trust you.

LARRY. Well, I'm about to make a scientific discovery.

FOREWOMAN. (*Flatly*) So what! I'm about to take your furniture.

LARRY. Oh, no, you're not!

FOREWOMAN. Can you give me one good reason why I ain't?

LARRY. I have a very good friend who's an extremely clever scientist.

REX. (*Making a face*) Ow!

FOREWOMAN. Your underslung pal either disagrees with you or he's got something in his stomach that disagrees with him.

LARRY. Don't pay any attention to Rex. No one does.

FOREWOMAN. (*Looking* REX *over*) Rex? Huh! I had a dog by that name once.

REX. (*Bridling*) Are you calling me a dog?

FOREWOMAN. I sure am! What you gonna do about it?

REX. (*Meekly*) Please may I scratch a flea, ma'am? (*He does so.*)

FOREWOMAN. (*Turning to* LARRY) Let's hear about your scientific friend. (*Forcefully.*) And just because I said I used to be with a circus don't get the idea that I don't know nothin' about scientists, because I do. I knowed Edison well enough to call him Albert.

REX. If you called Thomas Alva Edison "Albert" you must have been bosom pals.

LARRY. I think I'd better talk with your boss in the morning.

FOREWOMAN. Oh, no, you don't! That's just another one of your stalls.

REX. (*Sarcastically*) We call 'em ROOMS in this house. (*Sweetly.*) Aren't you thinking about that BARN you used to live in?

FOREWOMAN. (*Rolling up her sleeves*) So help me Hannah! I'm gonna make you into either a man or a mouse. (*Starts for* REX *who retreats behind* BILLIE.)

BILLIE. (*Contemptuously*) Better try the MAN first. After all, a mouse is a mouse and there's no changing him.

LARRY. Listen! I have the *proof* to present to your boss.

FOREWOMAN. (*Uncertainly*) Well, I dunno!

LARRY. (*Persuasively*) This fellow inherited his father's genius and worked under the direct tutelage of his uncle, both of them very well known. I really and truly have the proof of what I say.

FOREWOMAN. (*Still a bit uncertain*) W-e-l-l, O. K. But I'll say as Abraham Washington said: You can fool part of me all the time, all of me part of the time, but you can't fool all of me all the time, so help me Hannah.

REX. I particularly remember that "So help me Hannah" that he stuck on the end of that.

LARRY. (*Seeing that he is gaining his point*) Not only do I have printed proof in the matter of clippings and letters of recommendation but, if you insist, I am in a position to introduce you to the scientist himself.

REX. (*In a prayerful tone*) Oh, Mr. Barnum! How right you were! Not only is one born every minute, with two to take him, we're even gazing on twin suckers encased within one torso.

FOREWOMAN. (*Suspiciously, as she eyes* REX) Your underslung side-kick seems to be a little mite skeptical over this hermetical scientist.

LARRY. (*Glaring at* REX) Don't mind him. He's a born skeptic.

FOREWOMAN. Oh, yeah? (*To* REX.) Well, just take a little bicarbonate of sody. That'll settle your stomach. I ought to know as my great-aunt Hepatica on my foster father's stepfather's side of the house was always having trouble with disceptia and that always fixed her.

REX. It should!

(*Women's voices are heard off* R. *and all turn to face door.* CONNIE, ORPHA *and* AUNT RACHEL *enter.* AUNT RACHEL *is a vivacious woman of forty, who looks thirty and acts twenty-one. She is attractive, knows it, and has an outstanding personality. She wears a smart street dress with tasty bits of costume jewelry.* CONNIE *enters first and goes down* R., ORPHA *backstage* R. *This leaves* AUNT RACHEL *with a clean sweep to the* FOREWOMAN *who is facing* LARRY C. AUNT RACHEL, *true to type, makes a talking entrance.*)

RACHEL. Oh, I've never been so *utterly thrilled* in my life. Where is this *devastatingly charming* young backwoods Romeo you've been telling me about?

CONNIE. He *was* upstairs ——

(LA REINA *appears in door* L.)

RACHEL. (*Pointing dramatically at* FOREWOMAN) Oh, THERE he is! You don't have to tell Rachel, she knows. He has that aura of the wilds, that woodsy tang hanging over him, that halo of naturalness. Why, just to look at him one can tell at a glance he's one of nature's own. (*She advances toward the* FOREWOMAN.)

(*All stare in consternation but none is nearly as perturbed as the* FOREWOMAN *herself who starts backing hastily and bumps into* LARRY.)

LA REINA. She no look where she go again, Senor Larry. She is SUCH a goer-no-looker!

LARRY. (*Embracing* FOREWOMAN *to keep from falling*) Whoa, there!

FOREWOMAN. (*Angrily*) Unhand me! Who do you think you are anyway? Samson and his Dandelion?

REX. (*Snickering*) I'll bet you'd be a dandy lion on a date.

RACHEL. How quaint! Attired in coveralls and an old cap. How like a woodsy hermit.

FOREWOMAN. Quaint my eye! I believe in bein' practical and cheap.

REX. Sister! You described yourself to a T.

FOREWOMAN. (*Turning on* REX) Do I understand you're callin' me CHEAP?

REX. (*Frightened*) No! I—I——

RACHEL. Never mind him. Let me see the color of your eyes.

FOREWOMAN. (*Roughly as she faces* RACHEL) They're green 'n' black with pink trimmin's. (*Shoves face within an inch of* RACHEL'S.) Is that O. K. by you, sister?

RACHEL. (*In amazement*) Oh, good heavens! Your hermit isn't a man, girls! He's a woman!

CONNIE. We tried——

RACHEL. Oh, my goodness! Water! Water! (*Staggers and* ORPHA *and* LA REINA *run to help her. They then assist her, half-fainting, off* L.)

FOREWOMAN. (*Glaring around*) Will someone please tell me what this is all about?

LARRY. (*Placatingly*) Merely a case of mistaken identity. Now if you'll be so good as to go back to your office and tell your employer that I have the proof of my contentions ——

FOREWOMAN. (*Bluntly*) I ain't interested in none of your old contentions. What I want to know is, can you prove what you say?

LARRY. I certainly can.

REX. (*Warningly*) Gosh, Larry! You're sticking your neck out a mile.

LARRY. (*With a warning glare to* REX *and then a pleasant smile to the* FOREWOMAN) I believe that is all.

FOREWOMAN. Yeah? When you gonna see the boss?

LARRY. The first thing in the morning.

FOREWOMAN. W-e-l-l, I dunno! (*She looks at her helpers who have been taking all this in without a flicker of interest.*)

LARRY. You can trust my word.

FOREWOMAN. Yeah? Since when?

LARRY. (*Persuasively*) You KNOW you can.

FOREWOMAN. That's what you hope.

(*Doorbell heard off* R. *and* LA REINA *appears in door* L.)

CONNIE. Attend to your work, Queenie. I'll get it.

[LA REINA *exits* L. *as* CONNIE *goes out* R.

FOREWOMAN. (*Shrewdly*) You expectin' some other company after the rest of your compliances?

LARRY. No, no! Just some friends.

SUE. (*Off* R.) No! I have to see him personally.

CONNIE. (*Off* R.) I'm not sure he's here. Can't you tell me the nature of your business?

SUE. (*Off* R.) All I can tell you is that I'm a representative of the Skinem Insurance Company and ——

REX. (*His exclamation drowning the rest of* SUE's *words*) Ouchy wow-wow! The Skinem Insurance Company. (*Excitedly starts running in circles.*) I hope you folks'll pardon me while I find a place to hide.

LARRY. (*Puzzled*) What in the world are you hiding from?

REX. You would ask me that.

BILLIE. There you go! Running again!

REX.   It's either run or face a suit.

LARRY.   What kind of a suit?

REX.   (*Making for door* L.)   Don't ask so many blamed questions, Larry.   (*Stops at door as he hears* SUE *speaking.*)

SUE.   (*Off* R.)   No!   I can't state my business to any-one but Rex Simonds in person.

BILLIE.   (*Sarcastically*)   Not "in person" but in a quickie movie.

REX.   (*Groaning*)   I knew it!   Rex Simonds is little me, affectionately yours.   Good-bye!   [*Darts off* L.

(CONNIE *enters* R. *followed by* SUE, *an average girl attired for business duties.   She carries a small case under her arm, bulging with papers.*)

CONNIE.   (*Speaking as she enters and looking carefully around for* REX)   Very well, if you MUST come in but I'm sure Mr. Simonds left just a few moments ago.

BILLIE.   As of this minute.   He hied himself hence with amazing rapidity through yon library door.   (*Motions* L.)

LARRY.   (*Interrupting* BILLIE *hastily as he glares at her*)   Yes, he left all of a minute ago.   I'm sure he's —— I mean he'll be sorry he missed you.

SUE.   He'll be plenty sorry if I don't find him.

CONNIE.   Can't you tell us what business you wish to discuss with him?

FOREWOMAN.   All this can wait.   I——

CONNIE.   We might be willing to tell —— I mean we might be able to locate him if it's urgent.

FOREWOMAN.   My business is urgent but——

SUE.   Do you know when he'll be back?

BILLIE.   He'll be back just as soon as you've g——

LARRY.   (*Hastily*)   Yes!   I mean, No!   That is, we're not exactly sure when he'll be back.   You see, Rex sort of comes and goes.

FOREWOMAN.   (*Glancing toward door* L.)   Particularly goes.

LARRY.   And then he comes back and one can't really

say just when he might come back or when he might go.

BILLIE. Yes. He sorta mixes 'em up.

SUE. I see! (*But she doesn't.*) Well, I suppose I might give you a hint as to the nature of the business.

CONNIE. Of course. We'll keep it confidential.

SUE. He was involved in a traffic accident night before last and ——

LARRY. (*Sharply*) Traffic accident!

SUE. Yes.

LARRY. Did you say night before last?

SUE. Yes, I did.

LARRY. Was he in a car?

SUE. Of course.

LARRY. Was the car he was driving damaged?

SUE. Yes, quite badly. You see ——

LARRY. (*Grimly and with meaning*) Yes, I see a lot that I haven't seen before.

CONNIE. You don't mean it was your car?

LARRY. (*Angrily*) That's exactly what I do mean. (*Glaring toward door* L.) So! My car developed an ailment, did it, Rexxie, old boy.

BILLIE. (*On the defense for* REX) Hadn't you better get the details from him, Larry, before you ——

LARRY. Sure! That's probably *all* I'll get from him. I'll get the few details of my car that are left.

CONNIE. (*To* SUE) Do you want to serve a summons on Mr. Simonds?

LARRY. I hope!

SUE. There's to be a court hearing and ——

LARRY. (*With deadly calm*) He'll be there. Of course he may not be seeing anything but he'll be there.

SUE. But I have to see him in person first.

LARRY. If *I* get to him first there won't be any person.

SUE. (*Persistently*) Are you SURE he isn't around?

CONNIE. (*Interrupting* LARRY *who is about to speak*) No, he's not, but we'll tell him you're looking for him.

LARRY. (*Angrily*) As if having these—these talking penguins (*glares at* FOREWOMAN *and her helpers*) trying to hook the furniture isn't enough, little Rexxie boy has to go out and smash my car.

SUE. I think I smell a mouse.

FOREWOMAN. A mouse? It's smell enough for a *horse*.

LARRY. You do smell a mouse. When you rang the doorbell he left so quickly he left his scent behind him.

CONNIE. (*Placatingly to* SUE) Don't pay any attention to him. He's mad.

LARRY. Oh, no! I'm not mad! I just feel the need of going on a mouse-meat diet. I'll swallow him without even chewing.

BILLIE. (*Giggling*) I'll bet that would be fun for Rex.

FOREWOMAN. (*Addressing her helpers*) Well, we've had a free show. Now let's get this furniture outta here. Pick up your seat and walk.

LARRY. (*As helpers arise from divan*) Wait! You can't take that furniture.

(*As soon as* LARRY *starts his argument the helpers look at one another, shrug in unison and resume seats on divan.*)

FOREWOMAN. And just what's the reason I can't?

BILLIE. You don't own it. It's ours.

FOREWOMAN. That's what *you* think.

CONNIE. Why do you have to be so stubborn? My brother told you about this scientist who can work marvels.

FOREWOMAN. I ain't takin' no words from any of you. Look at what happens when I start gettin' soft. In walks a Skinem from an insurance company.

SUE. (*Resentfully*) Skinem is part of the name of our company.

FOREWOMAN. Yeah and I'm too much of a lady to repeat the rest of it.

LARRY. I give you my word of honor ——

FOREWOMAN. (*Snorts*) Honor! You stand there and yell about honor. You who stood here and let that little warty sidekick of yours run out on this woman when all she wants to do is sue him for an accident! Huh! Honor my foot.

BILLIE. Be reasonable! I know you don't look reasonable but do you have to be the way you look?

FOREWOMAN. I'm done argufyin'! Grab them household compliances, girls, and let's get outta here.

CONNIE. (*Rushing to the four girls as they rise*) You can't do that!

(LA REINA *has heard the commotion and enters* L. *looking on.*)

FOREWOMAN. You and who else is gonna keep us from doin' it?

CONNIE. Larry has a chance to get his inheritance now, a real chance. You can't take this furniture away and leave us with an empty house.

BILLIE. (*Joining* CONNIE) You'll have a fight on your hands if you try to take this stuff.

LA REINA. (*Also stepping in front of divan*) Si! Si! You no take muebles! We got the ermitano! This ermitano he got the invencion and this invencion will get us the dinero!

SUE. (*A bit frightened*) What in the world is wrong?

(*Next two speeches are spoken rapidly and alternately.*)

BILLIE. Don't you dare touch that furniture. We really have a scientist now. He's a good friend of my brother.

CONNIE. If you do I'll tear your hair out. And maybe one of us will marry him. He'll do anything for a friend.

LARRY. (*Yelling*) Listen, you two. This hubbub isn't getting us anywhere. Be quiet! Listen to me!

REX. (*Enters* L.) Hey! What's going on in here?

LA REINA. Mister Rex! They try to take the muebles.

REX. Let 'em have 'em. None of us wants any pebbles anyhow.

LARRY. She means furniture, you sap.

REX. Don't you call Rex Simonds a sap! You ——

SUE. Oh! Are you Rex Simonds?

REX. What? (*Faces* SUE.) Oh, my gracious goodness me! I thought you'd gone! Old Skinem! (*Bolts for door* R.)

LARRY. (*Grabbing him*) Listen, pimple! I want to talk to you.

REX. Well, I don't want to talk to you, not while you're in this mood! (*Jerks loose from* LARRY *and dashes off* L.)

LARRY. (*Glaring after him*) He *should* run!

SUE. Don't just stand there! Catch him! This is very important.

LARRY. When I'm done with him he won't be interested in anything you have to say.

SUE. But it's important to you, too.

LARRY. You're darned tootin'! But I'll wait to get at him.

(*The* FOREWOMAN *and helpers have stopped to watch this by-play but now resume their work with the furniture.*)

BILLIE. (*Grabbing the* FOREWOMAN) Larry! They're taking the furniture!

CONNIE. (*Trying to pull the four helpers away from divan*) Don't stand there like a big goof! *Do* something.

LA REINA. Si, Senor Larry. Something you must do and quick!

LARRY. (*To* FOREWOMAN) Now look here! I've explained our situation sufficiently.

FOREWOMAN. (*Trying to get loose from* BILLIE) Not to me you ain't.

LARRY. What do you expect me to do? Draw pictures?

FOREWOMAN. That's probably the only way you'll get money to pay for your furniture.

(ORPHA *and* AUNT RACHEL *enter* L., *stopping in amazement when they view the scene in room.*)

RACHEL. What's going on here?

ORPHA. Looks like the fighting front at a bargain sale.

CONNIE. They're trying to steal our furniture.

FOREWOMAN. (*Resentfully*) We ain't nuther! We're just *takin'* it.

LARRY. (*Starting for* FOREWOMAN) Like fun you're taking it.

RACHEL. They're taking it away from you just when you get that lovely, big, backwoods Romeo for a scientist?

ORPHA. Oh, you can't! Not now!

FOREWOMAN. (*Grimly*) We're takin' it even if we have to lug the house off with it. I'll learn you people that our contract for household compliances means just what it says! (*To helpers.*) Take it away!

> (*Helpers again start for divan as* FOREWOMAN *goes for a chair. All, save* SUE, *immediately surround them and prepare to do battle for the furniture. At this moment* ROMEO *appears on stairs with a small egg-like gadget in his hand. He draws arm back with gadget in hurling position.*)

ROMEO. Stop! I command you to cease this ridiculous display of animalistic emotionalism!

LARRY. (*Yelling*) Romeo! They're taking the furniture.

ROMEO. (*Calmly*) Indeed? (*Looks around.*) Who is the leader of this band of renegades?

FOREWOMAN. I ain't got no idea what them words means and I ain't got no band either. (*Steps toward stairs.*) What can I do for you?

ROMEO. Cease this infantile display of acrobatic wordage, which, I must say, is reminiscent of a juvenile delinquent.

FOREWOMAN. (*Suspiciously*) Are you tryin' to make a monkey outta me?

BILLIE. That would be as easy as making a whistle out of a pig's tail.

FOREWOMAN. (*Whirling angrily on* BILLIE) Did you call me a whistle?

BILLIE. No, I didn't call you a whistle. Now do you get it? The inference I mean?

FOREWOMAN. Listen! I ain't takin' no inference from you or anyone else. My boss said, " Get them compliances and if you get interference, just call the cops."

That's what my boss said and that's what I'm gonna do.

REX. (*Dashes in* L.) Larry! I just had to come back. I don't care what happens to me as long as you ——

LARRY. (*Menacingly*) Neither do I.

REX. (*Pleading*) Listen, pal! I'm risking my neck to come back here and tell you you're nuts to pin all your faith in goofy Romeo Montague. That guy's no more of a scientist than I am.

ROMEO. (*Stiffly from stairs*) Are you by chance referring to me, Mr. Simonds?

REX. (*Who has not seen* ROMEO *before*) Oh-oh and a couple of goshes!

LARRY. (*Walking toward* REX) What's this drivel you're dribbling over your chin? Come on! Prime your tonsils and come up with a logical answer or so help me ——

SUE. (*To* REX) You're Rex Simonds, aren't you?

REX. And you're old Skinem's right-hand female yesman, aren't you?

SUE. I have to deliver a message to you in person.

REX. Oh-oh! A summons for Simonds! (*Backs toward door* L.)

FOREWOMAN. (*To helpers*) Never mind these chattering magpies! They keep talkin' but never say nuthin'! Get them compliances outta here, girls.

(*All rush for the girls as they again take hold of divan.*)

ROMEO. (*Still on stairs*) STOP!

REX. What the heck do you think you have there?

ROMEO. An A-B-C-D bomb!

REX. Sure we see de bomb. What about it?

ROMEO. (*Balancing bomb in hand*) Beside this implement of destruction which you perceive balanced so precariously upon my upturned digits, all known atomic destructive forces are as bits of straw tossed upon the angrily foaming crests of hurricane lashed surf.

LARRY. (*Nervously*) We'll take your word for it. Get on with your fairy tale.

Romeo. You must comprehend that this is not a tale.

Rex. We can see that. You said it was a bomb.

Romeo. Of course you are not conversant with the theories and practises of nuclear physics; however ——

Rex. If that dinkus is half as powerful as you claim, we don't need any knowledge of physics to ——

Larry. (*Irritably*) Pipe down, dunce!

Romeo. (*Continuing*) Neither, of course, are common laymen like yourself familiar with cosmic rays, deuterons, cyclatrons, electrons, neutrons, positrons, ionization, radioactivity, transmutation, uranium or plutonium.

Forewoman. (*Whose jaw has dropped lower and lower as* Romeo *speaks*) Great jumpin' ginger! (*To* Larry.) Is that your scientist friend?

Rex. It isn't a real bomb. He's throwing a line.

Romeo. (*Ready to toss bomb at* Rex) Would you like a demonstration?

Rex. (*Yelling as he backs away*) No! No! Hey! You might be telling the truth and just in case you are, DON'T THROW THAT THING.

Billie. (*Sarcastically*) You great big strong he-man.

Rex. If a regular A bomb blew Hiroshima and Nagasaki off the map, what do you think a super-annuated physic like he's got would do to dear old home sweet home?

Larry. Romeo! These gals from the furniture company don't believe you're a real scientist. How can we prove that you are?

Rex. (*Warningly*) Don't encourage the guy, Larry.

Romeo. (*Calmly*) To prove my status in the field of scientific research, I could merely hurl this little implement of destruction and ——

All. (*Much excited*) No! No! Don't throw it! Please! (*Etc.*)

(La Reina *screams at top of her voice and exits* l.)

Rex. That thing could blow us all into Kingdom Come!

Larry. I thought you branded him as a fake.

REX. I could have gotten hold of the wrong branding iron, couldn't I?

FOREWOMAN. How am I to know you ain't just bluffin' us with that tomato you've got in your flipper?

ROMEO. (*With a tossing motion*) Would you care to catch this?

FOREWOMAN. (*Frightened*) Heavens, NO!

LARRY. (*Quickly*) Then you believe he *is* a scientist?

FOREWOMAN. (*Wiping her brow with a bandana*) Yeah, sure! I'll take his word for it.

LARRY. (*Pressing his point*) Then you'll promise to let the furniture stay here until I can speak with your boss in the morning?

FOREWOMAN. (*Nervously*) Yeah, sure, O. K.!

ROMEO. By those monosyllabic utterances am I to infer that it is your intention to imply your willingness to discontinue pestering Mr. McNeil this evening?

FOREWOMAN. I don't know just what you said but it's sure okie dokie with me. Just don't start experimentin' with that thing while I'm around.

LARRY. Then I'll bid you all good day and tell your boss that I'll see him in the morning.

FOREWOMAN. Come on, girls! (*The four helpers cross to her.*) I'll tell him what you said, only he ain't a him, he's a her.

LARRY. And thank you for all the trouble you've caused me.

FOREWOMAN. Don't thank me, thank that A to Z tomato your scientific palsy walsy's got tucked in his mitt. (*Quickly to* ROMEO.) Don't take no defense, Mister. I didn't say what I meant. Good night! (*To* LARRY *direct.*) That thing had better be good!

LARRY. (*Confidently*) It will be.

FOREWOMAN. (*Stops in door* R., *surrounded by her helpers*) It looks like a hand grenade. If that's all it is, brother, you'd better start in easy-like sprinklin' gunpowder instead o' sugar on your cereal in the mornin', because me 'n' the boss'll be feedin' you explosives and you'd better get your suggestive system used to 'em.

Come on, girls! (*Exits* R., *followed by her helpers, all watching them off.*)

REX. (*Suddenly looking at* SUE *at the same time she looks expectantly toward him*) I just happened to think.

BILLIE. (*Witheringly*) With what?

REX. I wanted to have a real talk with those furniture movers.

SUE. Mr. Simonds, I have ——

REX. Sure! I know you have to go and I for one am doing nothing to stop you.

SUE. That isn't what I started to say and you know it. I have some papers here that ——

REX. Don't I know it! (*Quickly.*) I mean, have you? I mean, I've got to get out of here. (*Goes* R., SUE *following him.*)

SUE. They're legal papers and ——

REX. (*Still backing from her*) I'd never have guessed if you hadn't told me.

LARRY. (*To* REX) I don't have any legal papers but I've got a good lethal punch waiting for you for wrecking my car.

REX. (*Still trying to avoid* SUE) I can explain all about that, Larry. It wasn't my fault at all.

LARRY. (*Stepping between* REX *and* SUE) So! It wasn't your fault! If it wasn't how does it happen that the Skinem Insurance Company sends a girl here to serve you with a summons?

REX. Will you tell me how they could do anything honest with a name like Skinem?

SUE. (*Indignantly*) I'll have you understand there is nothing dishonest about it or I wouldn't work for them.

LARRY. It isn't a question of honesty, it's a matter of ethics.

REX. Do you call it ethical to beat me up?

LARRY. (*Grimly*) It might not be ethical but it would be plenty enjoyable.

REX. (*A little courage at last*) And what do you think I'd be doing while you're beating me up?

BILLIE. Huh! That's easy! You'd be running.

REX. You keep out of this.

ORPHA.   After all, Larry, you should give Rex a chance to state his case.

REX.   (*Desperately*)   And, for gosh sakes, believe what I say.

RACHEL.   I'm sure Rex didn't intend to wreck your car, Larry.

REX.   (*Gratefully*)   Of course I didn't.

LARRY.   And a moron doesn't intend to look like a fool but he usually does.

REX.   Do I understand you to infer that I'm a moron?

LARRY.   It was more than inference and you know it.

REX.   Oh, I do, do I?

LARRY.   (*Stepping right up to* REX)   Positively!   Now what are you going to do about it?

REX.   (*Weakly*)   Well, I just wanted to make sure I understood what you meant.

BILLIE.   (*Disgustedly*)   You little coward!

REX.   Will you please stop complimenting me?   My ego can't stand it.

LARRY.   You still have some explaining to do about my car.

REX.   I didn't wreck your car.

LARRY.   What do you mean, you didn't wreck it?

REX.   Just what I say, *I* didn't wreck it.

LARRY.   You were driving it, weren't you?

REX.   (*Swallowing with difficulty*)   Yup!

LARRY.   You were sitting behind the wheel when the accident occurred, weren't you?

REX.   (*Again swallowing*)   Yup!

LARRY.   Then it was your fault, wasn't it?

REX.   (*Who is in the rut*)   Yup!   (*Instantly catches himself.*)   No!   NO!   It wasn't!

LARRY.   Well!   Make up your mind.

REX.   *NO!*

LARRY.   No what?

REX.   (*Stammering*)   No, yes!   I mean Yes, no!   I mean that the " Yes " I said was supposed to be a no and the " No " I said was supposed to mean yes.   I was NOT responsible for the accident.   Now do you know what I mean?

LARRY. (*Forcefully*) *NO!*
REX. Er—you don't?
LARRY. *I don't!*
ORPHA. Such silly arguing gets you no place and *fast!*
BILLIE. And if Larry keeps on scaring the poor little old " fraidy-cat " out of the few wits he has, he'll probably have a nervous breakdown.
REX. (*Turning angrily to* BILLIE) You listen to me, my fine feathered, frilly, frothy and flighty female ——
RACHEL. (*Reprimandingly*) Ah! Ah! Ah! That's enough, children. (*Looks around brightly.*) My! What a large evening. Orpha! Let's go out into the kitchen and brew ourselves a cup of tea.
ORPHA. After this I could use one.
LARRY. I want to have a talk with you, Orpha, before you go.
ORPHA. (*Turning to look at* ROMEO *who, standing upstage, has been watching the others with interest*) You'd better hurry up, Larry darling, or (*with a coy glance at* ROMEO) it might be too late.
LARRY. We'll see about that. (*Glares at* ROMEO.)
BILLIE. (*To* ORPHA) Hey! How do you get that way? He's my little backwoods Romeo!
REX. (*Angrily*) Is that so!
BILLIE. If you had the brain to concoct a bomb and then had the nerve to hold a whole crowd at bay with it —— (*Shrugs.*) Perhaps I MIGHT condescend to accept a date with you, *Mr.* Simonds.

(RACHEL *and* ORPHA *start* L., BILLIE *following.*)

REX. (*Following* BILLIE) That blamed thing might have blown us all to the Little Dipper and back. That blamed romance-rusted Romeo knew that. What he did didn't take any nerve.
BILLIE. (*Loftily*) Perhaps, but you had your chance to prove that you had nerve. I noticed you didn't try to take the thing away from him. (*Grins at* REX *and exits* L. *with* ORPHA *and* RACHEL.)

(ROMEO *looks after* BILLIE *in amazement and* REX *is too stunned to speak.*)

REX. (*With outraged dignity*) Did you hear that? (*Sputtering.*) Why—why, an atomic bomb has universal power back of it and that little—flip has the nerve to tell me I hadn't the nerve to take the thing away from him. (*Glares at* ROMEO *and then starts* L.) She sure has her nerve telling me I have no nerve.

LARRY. You're so well in practice defending that nerve you don't possess, suppose we get to the bottom of this car wreck.

REX. Can't we just forget the blamed thing? I was at the bottom of the darned thing when it happened.

LARRY. Then you should know exactly what took place.

REX. I'm as innocent as a baby lamb.

LARRY. Yeah! A BLACK one.

SUE. (*Interrupting as* REX *starts to answer*) Mr. Mc-Neil! Perhaps I can throw a little light ——

LARRY. Fine! Go ahead and throw a little light. Then I'll be able to see the pieces better when I take this little runt apart bit by bit.

REX. (*Backing toward door* L.) Honestly, I can explain it all, Larry.

LARRY. (*Slowly following him*) I'm listening.

REX. Do you have to listen so *loud?* (*Backs into chair, scrambles madly out of it and goes behind it.*)

LARRY. *You smashed my car!*

REX. I didn't, Larry, honestly I didn't.

LARRY. (*Roaring*) I know you didn't do it *honestly.* I just want to know the crooked means you used in doing it.

REX. Trusting soul, aren't you? (*To* SUE.) Will you stop looking at me as if I were the canary just before the cat swallowed it?

SUE. But I have good news for you, Mr. Simonds.

REX. (*Groans*) That's the last straw. Here I am about to be chewed up and spit out by a brother-in-law I haven't got and you have the nerve to stand there and gargle about a summons being good news. I suppose you'd say my obituary was fair news and that—that —— WHAT would be your idea of *bad* news?

CONNIE. This has gone far enough! The car is wrecked. You'll have to take it and like it, Larry.

LARRY. No, I won't like it. (*To* REX.) As for you, my fine feathered little fowl, you're going to get the stuffing beaten out of you and you'll take it and like it.

REX. But—but you can't do that!

ROMEO. I hope you'll excuse my intrusion into your conversation. I realize that it is an unpardonable breach of etiquette but it pains me deeply to see friends having enmity toward one another.

CONNIE. He's right, boys.

ROMEO. (*Much to the consternation of others idly tosses bomb from one hand to the other*) I realize it would be unseemly to encroach upon your hospitality to the extent that I was to threaten you with this bomb but should this altercation proceed to further bitterness I would be unable to restrain my ——

REX. (*Desperately*) Now wait a minute, Romie! You're tossing that thing around like a rubber ball.

ROMEO. (*Still tossing bomb back and forth*) It's perfectly safe, I assure you, if I do not make a miscalculation and drop it.

REX. Miscalculation? (*To others.*) The guy's nuts.

ROMEO. (*Smiling*) I presume you are indulging in some more of that odious jargon you call " sling."

REX. Oh! So you think slang smells, eh?

LARRY. He didn't say *odorous*, you dunce.

REX. I don't care what he said. I'm getting out of here. (*Darts toward door* L.)

SUE. Mr. Simonds! Please don't run away. I told you I have GOOD news for you. (*Crosses to him.*)

REX. Just because my last name is Simonds, don't get the idea that my first one is Simple. [*Exits* L.

SUE. (*Following him*) Wait, Mr. Simonds, wait!

LARRY. (*Glaring after* REX) Either I'm going to get that car wreck straight or I'm going to decrease the number of his limbs by tying a few of them together. [*Exits* L.

CONNIE. (*With a smile*) Well! You and I—er—seem to be alone, Romeo?

ROMEO. Since I became aware of the fact that you are—er—one of those women, conversation seems difficult indeed.

CONNIE. (*Sitting on divan*) Oh! You don't like women?

ROMEO. (*Sitting beside her*) Frankly I don't know. You and your fellow women have given me no cause to *dis*like you. I—I find myself in a mental quagmire so to speak.

CONNIE. Are we so different from men?

ROMEO. N-n-no! In fact, you speak with a surprising amount of intelligence. (*Pockets bomb.*)

CONNIE. (*A bit alarmed*) Do you carry that thing in your pocket?

ROMEO. Of course! Why do you ask?

CONNIE. I was just thinking if a girl had a date with you —— But you don't make dates, do you?

ROMEO. Make dates? I thought they grew on palm trees.

CONNIE. (*Dryly*) Uh-huh! Palm trees and family trees.

ROMEO. (*Puzzled*) It is all so very strange. I mean the manner in which you utilize words. You speak fluent English, and yet somehow you manage to convey the impression that you are speaking an entirely different language.

CONNIE. Didn't the boys explain slang to you?

ROMEO. As a matter of fact, they did, but I must admit the jargon you call " slang " still eludes me.

CONNIE. I see. You don't know very much about women, do you?

ROMEO. Very little. Uncle Benvolio was most cryptic concerning them. Until I came here I thought women were pests.

CONNIE. (*Laughing*) You're not alone in that thought.

ROMEO. But Uncle Benvolio must have known ——

CONNIE. He probably knew too much. You of course know what marriage is?

ROMEO. Marriage? Uncle said it was a form of merger but I'm certain you folks have some entirely different definition for it. (*Sighs.*) Do you know, I'm beginning to lose faith in Uncle's accuracy.

CONNIE. Do you know that men and women fall in love with one another?

ROMEO. Don't be foolish. How in the world could a *man* fall in love with a *woman?*

CONNIE. Don't ask me but lots of them do.

ROMEO. Well! Well! It is most amazing.

CONNIE. (*With a mock shudder*) Unthinkable! (*Very seriously.*) And another thing; some women fall in love with men.

ROMEO. *That's* more easily understood.

CONNIE. (*Suspiciously*) Are you sure you're as innocent as you'd have one believe, but—of course you are. It's just the male ego coming to light instinctively.

ROMEO. (*Rises and walks* R.) So men and women fall in love with one another. (*Turns and faces* CONNIE.) What on earth happens after they fall in love?

CONNIE. (*Indifferently*) Oh, they sometimes kiss each other.

ROMEO. Kiss?

CONNIE. I said " kiss." You know—er—er—osculate.

ROMEO. You mean like a fan? (*Imitates motion of fan.*)

CONNIE. I could answer that one too—but I won't. Do you mean to stand there and tell me you don't know what a kiss is like?

ROMEO. Most assuredly I do not know. (*Eagerly.*) Do you?

CONNIE. W-e-l-l, as a matter of fact, I do.

ROMEO. (*Still more eagerly*) Will you show me how it's done?

CONNIE. Didn't you ever hear of modesty in women?

ROMEO. No! Do they have it?

CONNIE. The antics of some of them would leave you guessing.

ROMEO.   Then you'll be so kind as to show me what a kiss is?

CONNIE.   Well! This is what I would call a unique situation. (*Looks at him sharply.*) You sure you never saw a woman until you came here?

ROMEO.   Whom do you take me to be? Iago?

CONNIE.   I'm not sure. (*Quotes.*) " Even a rose by another name would smell ——" (*Her voice leaves it hanging.*)

ROMEO.   (*Prompting her*) "—would smell as sweet."

CONNIE.   (*With irony*) Until I get to know you a little better, we'll just say " would smell ——" Period.

ROMEO.   I do not mean to encroach upon your hospitality but your manners, actions and colloquialisms intrigue me. For instance this art of kissing.

CONNIE.   Who told you it was an art?

ROMEO.   (*Thoughtfully*) I cannot recall that anyone referred to it as actually an art but I assume, from your recent reference to the action, that it requires a given technique. You have kissed, of course?

CONNIE.   Are you kidding?

ROMEO.   Oh, no!

CONNIE.   Well, kissing isn't a thing that's done every day. I mean that it isn't done a great deal in—in public places.

ROMEO.   Only the two of us are present?

CONNIE.   That's right.

ROMEO.   Are more than two needed for a kiss? I mean would we need help?

CONNIE.   That depends entirely on you.

ROMEO.   Then two of us can do it?

CONNIE.   Yes, it has been done by two.

ROMEO.   (*Enthusiastically*) Excellent! I am ready to be shown.

CONNIE.   Willing, aren't you? (*Rises and faces him.*) Listen, big boy, if you think you're going to pull a fast one on me, you're ——

ROMEO.   " A fast one? "

CONNIE.   (*Sweetly*) Yes, dearie, because I'll bite your

nose off. Well, nothing risked, nothing won. First, you put your arms around my shoulders.

ROMEO. (*Not the least embarrassed, does so*) Is this the action to which you aspire?

CONNIE. I neither aspire nor perspire. I merely told you to do it; however, it's right.

ROMEO. (*Disappointed*) And is that what you call a kiss?

CONNIE. No, that's only the beginning, brother, only the beginning.

ROMEO. Oh! Then what must I do next, or is it your move?

CONNIE. (*Watching him closely*) I guess you really are dumb. Anyway, here goes. Now hold me close to you.

ROMEO. (*Very matter-of-factly*) This is a strange proceeding. Do you mean thus? (*Squeezes* CONNIE *very tightly.*)

CONNIE. (*Jerking away from him a bit*) Let's make it this. Thus is too hard! There! That's better. Now you place your lips on mine and that's a kiss.

ROMEO. (*Disappointed*) Really? (*Puzzled.*) What's the point to it?

CONNIE. None, if you don't automatically get it. (*Moves away from him.*) Now you know and ——

ROMEO. (*Following her*) One moment, please. I feel I should carry on and see if I can understand.

CONNIE. W-e-1-l, if you MUST. (*Holds her lips upward.*)

ROMEO. Merely TOUCH the lips!

(*She nods and he touches her lips with his. Then* CONNIE *slides her arm around his shoulders and really kisses him.*)

REX. (*Barging in hurriedly from* L.) Pardon me, folks, but I've got to hide before I lose my hide. That woman chased me clear around the block.

CONNIE. (*Embarrassed*) Oh! (*Breaks away from* ROMEO *and dashes off* L.)

(*She leaves* ROMEO *with eyes closed, weaving on his feet. He starts toward armchair* R. C. *but moves in an arc, misses armchair when he goes to sit and, still dazed, sits on floor. Even contact with the floor fails to bring him to.*)

REX. (*Looks at him puzzled then walks up to him*) Hey! What were you and Connie doing when I came in?

ROMEO. Er—I—ah ——

REX. (*Shaking him by shoulder*) What was going on?

ROMEO. (*Rises and gingerly sits in armchair*) We—er—Connie told me about the kiss and she was—er—kind enough to show me how it is done. (*Sighs.*) I've heard about dissipation in civilization but ——

REX. Dissipation?

ROMEO. Yes! Uncle Benvolio often mentioned the state of intoxication but this is the first time I ever experienced it myself.

REX. You mean that you think kissing Connie made you *drunk?*

ROMEO. That must be my ailment. I seem to have the rudimentary symptoms of inebriation. I am not ill yet, somehow I feel possessed. I have such a giddy sensation permeating my entire being.

REX. And you don't know why kissing Connie made you feel that way?

ROMEO. I can see no earthly reason for it.

REX. That, my friend, is because kissing is out of this world.

ROMEO. (*Thoughtfully*) I see! (*Rises.*) I trust you will excuse me, sir, but I suddenly have a strong desire to cogitate. (*Starts for stairs.*)

REX. Go to it, chum. I know just how you feel.

ROMEO. (*Pausing at foot of stairs*) You have felt thus after a kiss?

REX. You said it! I have felt thusly and so-ly! I've had cogitation, coagulation and—condemnation, all rolled

Romeo. Oh! Then there is nothing organically *wrong* with me?

Rex. Nope! If you didn't feel that way then I'd say there was.

Romeo. I see! (*But he doesn't. He starts upstairs but stops and turns.*) You don't have a book of slang about you, do you?

Rex. Of course not! What do you want with such a thing?

Romeo. I'm sorry you haven't one. Slang is so difficult to fathom.   [*Exits stairs.*

Rex. (*Goes to foot of stairs and looks after* Romeo) You don't know it yet, brother, but I think you're in love, and is THAT hard to fathom. (Billie *appears in door* L.) The language of slang. You should study the language of love.

Billie. And what do you know about the language of love, pinhead?

Rex. (*Wheeling to face her*) Oh! (*Meets her at divan.*) Won't you please defrost a bit, Billie?

Billie. (*Mimics him*) Won't you please starch your courage a bit, Rexie?

Rex. What do you expect of a guy in the jam I'm in?

Billie. Of a *real* guy, I would expect a little *courage*.

Rex. (*Bridling*) Meaning that I'm not a real guy?

Billie. If you are, you're the first mouse I ever met named Guy.

Rex. (*Angrily*) Listen, woman! I'm not going to stand here and listen to you run down my courage.

Billie. Your *what?*

Rex. I should take you across my knee and beat a little sense into your head.

Billie. (*Contemptuously*) That would be just about your speed, beating up a girl. (*Suddenly melting.*) Look, Rex! Your type's all right for me. (Rex *looks up eagerly.*) I mean the way you *look* but you act like such a scared cat all the time.

Rex. (*Resentfully*) I'll have you know that I'm not scared.

Billie. I often wish you weren't the way you are.

REX. (*Contritely*) I don't blame you. But how can I help being what I am? I guess my mother dropped me on my head when I was a baby.

BILLIE. And scared you for life? (*Scornfully.*) You should be ashamed. It just takes will power. (*Pleading.*) Why can't you be a man, Rex? I like you lots better than—Romeo, for instance, but he's a man so I guess I'll have to marry him instead of you.

REX. Billie! You—you mean you'd marry me if I got some courage?

BILLIE. I said I like your type. (*Shrugs.*) But it's no use. You can never pump up any courage.

REX. (*Bravely*) With you feeling that way toward me there's nothing on earth can scare me.

BILLIE. You mean you *will* be *brave?*

REX. From now on, baby, I'll eat centipedes on my cereal instead of sugar and when I need a fur coat I'll go out and catch a bear with my bare hands and wear him.

BILLIE. (*Soulfully*) Oh, Rex! I just love to hear you talk like that.

SUE. (*Enters* L.) Oh there you are, Mr. Simonds!

REX. Oh—oh! Old Skinem looking for a sucker named Simonds! (*Rushes off* R.)

SUE. (*Following him*) But, Mr. Simonds, I told you I have good news for you.   [*Also exits* R.

BILLIE. (*Glaring at door* R.) Says he'll wear a bear! He wouldn't even dare wear a tan.

REX. (*Dashes in* R.) How's that for giving old Skinem the slip? (*Dashes off stairs.*)

BILLIE. (*At foot of stairs angrily yells after him*) Look out you don't bump your toe on that courage you just dropped.

(LARRY *and* ORPHA *enter* L.)

ORPHA. I thought I heard Rex in here.

LARRY. He probably ran when he heard our footsteps.

BILLIE. (*With utter disgust*) He doesn't wait to hear

anything as heavy as footsteps. Little Rex can hear anyone cast a shadow.   [*Exits* L.

ORPHA. (*Looking after* BILLIE) She seems a bit upset.

LARRY. So will little Rex be upset if he doesn't pull a
good explanation out of his hat for wrecking my car.
But let's not talk about him, Orpha. I want to talk to
you about us.

ORPHA. What about us?

LARRY. W-e-l-l, I don't like the way you've been shin-
ing up to Romeo Montague.

ORPHA. (*Brightly*) Does it show?

LARRY. It certainly does.

ORPHA. I'm glad. I was afraid it wouldn't.

LARRY. (*Protesting*) But I thought you and I **were**
as good as engaged.

ORPHA. Did you ever propose to me?

LARRY. Well, no!

ORPHA. Did *I* ever propose to you?

LARRY. Of course not, but ——

ORPHA. Have we ever talked about marriage?

LARRY. No, but ——

ORPHA. Then we're not as " good as engaged." Perhaps good but definitely not engaged.

LARRY. But we're going to be married and ——

ORPHA. Yes? Who told you?

LARRY. I've always taken it for granted that ——

ORPHA. You should learn, Larry, not to take too much
for granted—especially a woman.

LARRY. (*A bit alarmed*) Do you mean that you won't
marry me?

ORPHA. No girl likes a man to take for granted she's
going to marry him without even the trouble of asking.

LARRY. I am asking you right now.

ORPHA. (*Indifferently*) I'm afraid you're a little late.

LARRY. Late? What do you mean?

ORPHA. (*Coyly*) I'll bet Romeo wouldn't take a girl
for granted.

LARRY. (*Stunned*) Romeo? Do you mean to stand

there and tell me you're in love with that backwoods woo-pitcher?

ORPHA. (*Dreamily*) My backwoods Romeo! Doesn't that sound romantic, Larry?

LARRY. Romantic? That nitwit doesn't even know there *is* such a thing as romance. (*Triumphantly.*) Why, he wouldn't even know how to kiss you.

ORPHA. That's what *you* think.

LARRY. Oh! And when did he ever learn how to kiss?

ORPHA. (*With a sigh*) This evening.

LARRY. (*Ominously*) And whom, may I ask, was his teacher?

ORPHA. Well, we girls were together and he offered the job to one of us.

LARRY. And then ——

ORPHA. I simply couldn't resist his child-like technique.

LARRY. (*Roaring*) Technique? That gaumbo hasn't any technique! One can't have technique without experience and he wasn't experienced when he came here.

ORPHA. (*Cautiously watching Larry*) He is now.

LARRY. (*Inarticulate for a moment*) Why—why—you—he —— I don't believe it! It's a lie—I hope!

ORPHA. (*Smiling*) Why don't you ask him?

(CONNIE, BILLIE *and* RACHEL *enter* L.)

RACHEL. My goodness! It's just you and Larry, Orpha. I thought someone had captured a lion when we heard that roaring.

CONNIE. What's wrong this time, Larry?

BILLIE. If you're looking for Rex and want to bring him out in the open just wave a piece of cheese around.

ORPHA. (*Winking secretly to* CONNIE) I was just telling Larry that Romeo gave a lesson ——

LARRY. I don't believe it.

CONNIE. It's true, Larry!

LARRY. WHAT!

REX. (*Heard off stairs*) Hey! The guy's nuts! (*Enters stairs as fast as he can without falling.*)

LARRY.　(*Disgustedly*)　What scared you this time?
A cricket?

REX.　It's that guy Romeo!

(ROMEO *appears at head of stairs.*)

LARRY.　What did he do now?

REX.　(*To* CONNIE)　You know that dressmaker's
manikin you have up in the hall?

CONNIE.　Of course but——

REX.　I just caught the guy kissing it!

LARRY.　(*Turns and glares at* ROMEO)　Is what he says
true?　(*Indicates* REX.)

ROMEO.　Yes and it's rather odd, you know.　I found
out that kissing that isn't at all the same as kissing a *real*
woman.

LARRY.　(*Grimly*)　Oh, so you *did* kiss a real woman,
did you?　(*Starts for* ROMEO *who is now at foot of
stairs.*)　Why, you double-crosser!　I thought you were
just an old backwoods Romeo and——

REX.　Look out, Larry.　He's liable to kiss you!

LARRY.　Yeah?　Well, I'll show him!　(*Grabs* ROMEO
by the collar and jerks him C.)

GIRLS.　(*All crowd around* LARRY *and try to prevent
him doing any injury to* ROMEO, *all speaking at once*)
Don't hurt him, Larry!　He's so innocent.　Larry, please!
Stop him, Rex!　Run, Romeo, run!　(*Etc.*)

(ROMEO *suddenly reaches in his pocket and withdraws
bomb.　All back away from him in terror.*)

ROMEO.　(*Turning to* LARRY)　Now just what was it
you wanted to show me, Mr. McNeil?

CURTAIN

ACT III

*(It is the same time of day as when the previous acts
opened and not only are the scenery and furnishings
the same, but the self-same furniture movers are at-
tempting to remove the same furniture as the curtain
opens. The workers have the room to themselves for
a brief moment and then La Reina enters L. When
she sees the movers she gives a loud yell of dismay.)*

La Reina. Ohhhhhh! It is you again and you take
our *muebles*! (*Yells at the top of her lungs.*) SENORS!
SENORAS! SENORITAS!

Forewoman. (*Who has been tugging armchair R. C. toward door R. stops and makes a face of distaste*) Of
course it couldn't be anyone else. It hadda be you and
after we sneaked in here so quiet like.

Helpers. (*All sit in a row on divan and start to sing*)
" It hadda be you! "

Forewoman. (*Furiously*) SHUDDUP!

*(The helpers exchange knowing glances, lift their
shoulders in unison, then settle comfortably back on
divan.)*

La Reina. You termite! I mean you *boss* termite!
Take these *peons* (*indicates helpers*) and away go you.

Forewoman (*Irritably*) Listen, you! Your boss
promised my boss that he'd pay for them compliances this
morning but your boss ain't never paid my boss one cent.
So if your boss ain't gonna pay my boss then it's my job
to see that the stuff is moved and with a capital moo!

La Reina. Mooooo yourself! (*Yelling.*) Senor
Larry! Senor Larry!

*(The helpers look at one another and again lift their
shoulders in unison.)*

Rex.   (*Entering* L.)   I've got a sneaking feeling I have no business walking into this mess.

Billie.   (*Immediately following him*)   You've been promising me you'd do something big, brave and strong. Now's your chance!   (*Shoves him toward* Forewoman.)

Rex.   I wonder why things are always so much worse when they happen NOW than when they happen THEN.

Forewoman.   (*Challengingly to* Rex)   Well?

Rex.   (*With a sickly smile*)   Oh, I'm well, thank you. How are you?

Forewoman.   FINE!   And I don't give a whoop how you are.   What do you want?

Rex.   (*Meekly pointing*)   Just the furniture, ma'am.

Billie.   (*Egging him on*)   Show her your mettle, Rex?

Rex.   My *mettle?*   (*Relieved.*)   Oh, you mean my *heel irons?*   (*Holds up shoe and points to rim of heel.*)   Here! Right here!

Larry.   (*Enters* R. *with* Orpha)   Ohhhh!   Let's go on, Orpha!   We've seen the show from here on.

Forewoman.   (*Turning to* Larry)   So *there* you are!

Larry.   And *there* you are.   What about it?

Forewoman.   You ain't come acrost with no money and you ain't come acrost with no inventor that can invent nothin'.

Rex.   " Nothin' " is a hard thing to invent.

Forewoman.   (*Whirling on him*)   You keep outta this.

Rex.   (*As* Sue *enters* R.)   Better advice has been given to no man.

Sue.   I hope you'll forgive me for barging in without ringing but it seemed the only way I'll ever successfully sneak up on Mr. Simonds.

Rex.   Oh-oh!   Skinem again with a summons for Simonds.   (*Starts* L.)

Billie.   (*Sticking out foot*)   No you don't!

(Rex *falls over the foot, falling flat on his face.*)

Rex.   (*From position on floor*)   You traitoress!

SUE.   (*Hurrying to* REX)   Stay right where you are, Mr. Simonds.

REX.   (*Sitting up*)   Here's where I get the book thrown at me.

LARRY.   Well!   What can you expect?   You took my car out and threw it at someone.

REX.   (*Rising to feet*)   I'll have you know, Larry McNeil, I didn't throw your car at anyone.   I was doing my best to observe the four freedoms and look what I get for it.

SUE.   I've been trying to tell you for two whole days, Mr. Simonds, that I have good news for you.

REX.   Isn't this hard enough for me?   Why do you keep building me up for a fall?

SUE.   (*Handing him paper*)   This will explain everything.

REX.   (*Trying to avoid paper*)   I can't read!   I don't know anything.

LARRY.   We'll all agree to that statement.

REX.   I'm innocent, I tell you.   The accident was forced on me.   I didn't disobey any traffic regulations and I obeyed every civil law in the book.   By golly, I even lived up to international law.

SUE.   I advise you to read that paper.

REX.   (*Closing his eyes and pushing paper toward* BILLIE)   You read it.   I haven't the heart to hurt myself so much.

BILLIE.   (*With a look of utter disgust takes paper*)   You great big overgrown baby!

REX.   (*Miserably*)   All I can say is that I'm innocent. If they hang me for this—well, a fellow can't keep from being hanged but I'll be hanged if I'll go to jail for what happened because I didn't do any wrong.

BILLIE.   (*Who has been reading paper*)   Why, Rexie, darling!

REX.   It's too late to start calling me " darling."   If I have to go to jail we can never be married anyhow.

FOREWOMAN.   All right, girls!   Let's ——

LARRY.   Never mind the accident.   If this keeps up we'll lose our furniture.

FOREWOMAN. You've already lost it, brother. We just gotta take it outta the house this time or we lose our jobs.

LARRY. Wait! I talked to your boss about a scientist.

FOREWOMAN. My boss don't think that geezer is a scientist. She thinks he's a impossible.

LARRY. Romeo Montague is not an impostor. How could he be when he's merely posing as himself and no one else?

FOREWOMAN. Don't ast me. All I know is what I'm paid for.

LARRY. I didn't just pull him out of a hat. I'm on the level. He's the real McCoy.

FOREWOMAN. (*Suspiciously*) I thought you said his name was Montague.

LARRY. It doesn't make any difference what his name is. He's a REAL scientist.

FOREWOMAN. W-e-1-1, I dunno.

LARRY. Your boss doesn't understand.

FOREWOMAN. (*Wavering*) I hate to go against my own buttered bread.

HELPERS. (*In unison*) *We won't!*

FOREWOMAN. (*Turning on them*) Shuddup!

LARRY. You've seen Romeo and your boss hasn't. Can't you judge a man by his looks?

FOREWOMAN. He sure is a good looker.

HELPERS. (*In unison*) *We'll say!*

FOREWOMAN. Shuddup!

LARRY. Coming right down to brass tacks, do you really believe that a man with a face like his *could* be a crook?

FOREWOMAN. (*Thoughtfully*) Brother! You got something there. He's sure got an honest mug. (*Dreamily.*) Yeah, it sure would be hard for me to believe that a guy as handsome as he is could be a livin' lie! (*Helpers all sigh deeply in unison.*) SHUDDUP!

LARRY. Would you feel more convinced if Romeo himself would tell you he's a real scientist?

FOREWOMAN. (*Smiling*) Sure! Let's have him in. Wouldn't mind havin' another look at him from close up.

(CONNIE *and* ROMEO *enter* R.)

LARRY. Just the man we want to see! (*The helpers all sigh deeply in unison while the* FOREWOMAN *smiles coyly at* ROMEO.) Romeo! You're just in time. I want you to tell this—lady (*glares at* FOREWOMAN) something.

CONNIE. That's why we came in. Romeo has something to tell everyone.

LARRY. (*Gleefully*) Swell! Swell! All right, Romeo! Shoot the works.

ROMEO. (*Staring blankly at* LARRY) I beg your pardon.

CONNIE. (*Gently*) He means for you to go ahead, Romeo.

ROMEO. Oh! (*Hesitantly.*) I hardly know how to begin. (*His head drops and he stares miserably at the floor.*) It—it is my humble obligation to confess that I fear I have misled all of you. This—this bomb—(*fumbles for it in his pocket*) is a failure.

LARRY. (*Who has been smiling confidently, suddenly loses his self-assurance*) What! A failure? Romie, you're spoofing.

REX. (*With morbid satisfaction*) I've been trying to tell you but you refused to listen to the words of wisdom I let dribble over my chin.

LARRY. (*Angrily*) You keep out of this! After your wrecking of my car behind my back I wouldn't take your word for anything.

(*Next two cues are given together.*)

BILLIE. But, Larry! Rex didn't ——
SUE. I've been trying to tell you ——
LARRY. (*Roaring*) Don't ever use that thing's name with mine. As of this minute I'm disowning him.

REX. Isn't that a bit of futuristic figuring? Disowning a brother-in-law before he gets to be one.

BILLIE. Rex, darling ——

REX. To iterate, appropriate and dissipate the phrases of your *big* brother, I say unto you: " You keep out of this."

BILLIE. (*Excitedly*) But, Rex, you don't realize what awfully ——

REX. When dealing with an insurance agent by the name of Skinem, nothing is too awful for me to realize.

SUE. (*Hotly*) I resent that! My company doesn't intend to do anything to you.

LARRY. Pipe down, ALL OF YOU!

CONNIE. Yes, please do. Romie hasn't completed his statement as yet.

LARRY. (*Gloomily*) I don't see what more he could have to say. (*Shrugs.*) Oh, well! Perhaps my hearing has gone bad. Just to make sure, Romie, will you kindly repeat what you said a moment ago?

REX. Sure! Repeat it, Romeo. Let someone else get heckled aside from me.

LARRY. Will you kindy close that tunnel you call a mouth?

REX. (*Indignantly*) If my mouth is a tunnel, what in the world do you call that quarry nature put in your face?

LARRY. (*Wearily*) O. K., Romeo, go ahead.

ROMEO. I simply made the statement that my bomb is a failure.

FOREWOMAN. And that's a-plenty! (*Triumphantly to* LARRY.) I told you I'd take his word for it. (*Faces her helpers.*) O. K., girls! We take 'em out now!

(*Helpers rise and wearily take hold of divan.*)

CONNIE. Larry! Make them wait a moment!

LARRY. I've waited too long already. If we hadn't this furniture so long, we wouldn't be accustomed to it and losing it wouldn't hurt so much, so they might as well take it.

CONNIE. But Romeo hasn't finished yet.

LARRY. Don't I know he hasn't? He may not know it yet but he's been assigned to the job of helping these— vultures ——

FOREWOMAN. (*Indignantly as helpers in unison turn and glare at* LARRY) Say, you ——

LARRY. (*Continuing*) —helping these vultures remove all of our furniture. (*Advancing menacingly on* ROMEO.) Come on, Don Juan Shakespeario! Shake a leg!

ROMEO. (*Looks at* LARRY *for an instant, then raises one leg and shakes it*) Is this the action you wish performed?

LARRY. (*Roaring*) *NO!* I want you to raise 'em *both* and shake 'em in unison.

(*There is a dead silence while everyone watches* LARRY *and* ROMEO. ROMEO *experiments for a moment then his shoulders slump and he looks hopelessly at* LARRY.)

ROMEO. It cannot be done.

CONNIE. Larry! You're being very unreasonable.

LARRY. Oh, am I? I suppose it was a perfectly normal procedure for him to throw Rex and me a·big line about his scientific achievements.

ROMEO. (*Quickly*) I beg your pardon. I never made any boasts as to my own achievements. I merely orally reviewed some practises of my late Uncle Benvolio.

LARRY. (*Dryly*) Those uncles surely come in handy, don't they? Why don't you go on the radio or television and make a few millions out of those fictional relatives of yours?

ROMEO. (*Sighing*) There have been times when I almost wished Uncle Benvolio had been fictional.

LARRY. That's enough! Now suppose you bend that scientific back of yours and lock onto that sofa with your breadhooks.

ROMEO. "Lock onto that sofa?" With my "breadhooks"?

CONNIE. (*Stepping between* LARRY *and* ROMEO) You've no right to talk this way, Larry, and I won't permit it.

LARRY. (*After a moment*) O. K.! We'll call Don Juan a guest and let it go at that. (*Whirls on* REX.) But you, my little crooked sonny-boy, don't come under that category. Get a move on before I fix you up for a veterinarian! (*Shoves him toward divan.*)

REX. Don't I even rate a helper?
LARRY. Helper! Get moving!
BILLIE. You leave Rex alone!
REX. The big bully!
LARRY. Are you going to start to move furniture or —— (*Raises his fist.*)
REX. (*Quickly*) I'll take the furniture. (*Goes to divan and starts to laboriously drag it toward door* R.)
FOREWOMAN. (*Delighted*) Well! That's what I calls service. Grab on, girls!

(*The helpers all grab other end of divan, leaving* REX *wrestle with his end alone. The* FOREWOMAN *picks up the smallest chair in the room and* LARRY *irritably rushes to the armchair.*)

LARRY. Grab a chair, Billie! You, too, Connie! We'll let the penguins get the rest.
BILLIE. (*Pleadingly*) But, Larry! I tell you you don't have to do this.
REX. (*Grunting painfully*) Don't argue with him! He thinks he needs to. Honest to gosh! I never saw a guy whose thinking was so loud and painful to others.
LARRY. Never mind my thinking. Get that thing out of the way.
REX. (*As he disappears through door with helpers*) It's going—whether you mean the sofa or me.
BILLIE. (*As* LARRY *staggers off* R. *with armchair*) I never saw such a dumb thing! (*Grabs piece of furniture.*) Oh, well, he'll learn. (*To* SUE.) Your man's out there. (*Nods* R.) Better grab a piece of furniture and follow him.   [*Exits with her piece of furniture.*
FOREWOMAN. (*To* SUE) Well! Get goin'!

(SUE *picks up piece of furniture and she and the* FOREWOMAN *exit* R.)

ORPHA. Well, La Reina, we might as well be in the swim. Let's grab!

(*They do so and each exits* R. *with a piece of furniture.*)

ROMEO. (*Goes to door* R. *and looks off, then turns and faces* CONNIE) Connie! I —— (*Catches himself.*) From what I hear, I presume I should address you as *Miss* McNeil!

CONNIE. Not at all! Connie is all right with me. What I want to know is, why didn't you tell Larry everything?

ROMEO. You'll forgive me for speaking with utter frankness?

CONNIE. (*Smiling*) Certainly.

ROMEO. It is difficult for me to adjust myself to the ways and manners of you folk. I am forced to admit that during great amounts of our conversation together I find myself utterly bewildered by your colloquialisms, mannerisms and general diction.

CONNIE. But diction is clear speech and we speak very distinctly.

ROMEO. I beg your pardon, but diction is one's manner of speaking, his choice of words and phrases. (*He pauses and smiles sheepishly.*) Of course I'm wrong again. You seem to have a different meaning for every word I ever learned.

CONNIE. Come to think of it, perhaps you're right, but let's not talk about that. Let's ——

ROMEO. Of course. Shall we talk about you—and me?

CONNIE. (*Surprised*) You and me?

ROMEO. Certainly. (*Seriously.*) I'd like to analyze the difference between us.

CONNIE. (*Cautiously*) Yes? What difference?

ROMEO. (*Embarrassed*) Our environment and—and —well, you see, I never realized that women had any reason at all.

CONNIE. (*Alert and on the defensive*) No?

ROMEO. (*Describing his ideas rather painfully*) You see Uncle Benvolio described women to me as being ugly, nonsensical, rather necessary but evil nonentities. On many an occasion he would snort with disgust and say they were dumb. (*Smiles.*) At the time I misinterpreted his meaning and took it for granted that women were a species of dumb animal.

CONNIE. Indeed!

ROMEO. Since coming here I realize to what Uncle was referring by his use of the term " dumb."

CONNIE. (*Belligerently*) You do! So Uncle Benvolio said women were dumb and now that you've met a few you've found out to your own satisfaction that what he said was true.

ROMEO. Oh, no, not at all! I thought he was referring to their inability to speak when actually, since coming here, I have found that he was employing a slang term.

CONNIE. (*Relaxing a little*) And what have *you* decided about women?

ROMEO. (*With a deep sigh*) I think they're *wonderful!*

CONNIE. Yes? *All* of them?

ROMEO. I've only met those connected with this household but you must believe me when I say that they are *above*.

CONNIE. Above? Oh! You mean tops?

ROMEO. I've always found foreign languages difficult.

CONNIE. (*Carefully*) Now that you've met several women, do you see any difference between them? (*He looks puzzled and she explains further.*) I mean, do *all* women appear *alike* to you?

ROMEO. Oh, no! I can readily distinguish you from any of the others.

CONNIE. I mean, do you *like* one woman more than you do another?

ROMEO. (*Seriously*) Do you know, you've brought up a very interesting matter. It's extremely odd but I think I do. (*Bewildered.*) I've been wondering if I'm normal. Somehow I feel awfully odd.

CONNIE. In what way?

ROMEO. I hardly know how to explain the sensations I have. (*Painfully shifting from one foot to the other.*) For instance: I don't feel the same toward men as I do toward women.

CONNIE. (*Having a hard time to hold back her laughter*) Really?

ROMEO. Really. When I meet men I seem to feel the same toward each of them.

CONNIE. And how do you feel when you meet women?

ROMEO. Well, I have an entirely different sensation for each woman I meet.

CONNIE. (*Grinning*) That *is* odd.

ROMEO. Take yourself, for instance. I don't feel the same toward you that I do toward the others I've met since my arrival.

CONNIE. I suppose you dislike me and that's what is so difficult to explain.

ROMEO. (*Hastily*) Oh, no! Most assuredly not. It's quite the contrary. Rex and Larry have intimated to me that it is apropos for a man and woman to fall in love with one another. So —— Why, you said the same thing!

CONNIE. There have been such cases on record.

ROMEO. (*Seriously*) Of course I realize this must seem strange to you but I am not conversant with the sensations which one must experience when he is mastered with the frailties which relegate him to the level of what is technically known as a lover.

CONNIE. (*Indignantly*) *Relegate* him? You speak as though it is *your* exalted opinion that one must lower himself into a—a sort of evil abyss before he can fall in love.

ROMEO. W-e-l-l, it is my belief that one must utilize what you might term the baser emotions.

CONNIE. (*Sarcastically*) Oh! You have it all figured out to a "T," haven't you? However, you interrupted yourself in the middle of a dissertation on how you feel toward me.

ROMEO. (*Earnestly*) I certainly feel differently toward you.

CONNIE. More *base*, I presume.

ROMEO. Oh, no! Quite the contrary, I assure you. I feel sort of—er—giddy.

CONNIE. (*Moving a bit toward him*) Giddy?

ROMEO. Y-yes. (*Looks at her a moment.*) There it comes again.

CONNIE. What?

ROMEO. That giddy feeling. I feel almost irresponsible. (*Puts hands on her shoulders and faces her.*) How do you feel?

CONNIE. (*Giggling*) Giddy!

ROMEO. Why, my hands feel as if they contacted an electrical current. (*Stares at* CONNIE *as though mesmerized.*) Is—is it contagious?

CONNIE. Is what contagious?

ROMEO. This emotion called love. I—I'm afraid I've caught it and if it's contagious I'm afraid you may contract it.

CONNIE. (*Demurely*) W-e-l-l, would that be such a tragedy?

ROMEO. (*Gradually putting his arm around her*) I feel positively contaminated with the bacteria of love. I —I'm having a terrific struggle within myself to avoid the re-enactment of our kissing demonstration.

CONNIE. (*More than willing*) Would you *like* to re-enact that scene?

ROMEO. What was it Uncle Benvolio used to say? (*Staring straight in* CONNIE'S *eyes.*) " Get thee behind me, Satan." " Get thee behind —— (*He kisses her.*) Mmmmmmmmm!

REX. (*Enters* R.) Oh! The show always seems to be fading out every time I come in.

(ROMEO *and* CONNIE *break apart sheepishly and one goes* R., *the other* L.)

ROMEO. (*Stammering*) We—we were re-enacting a scene ——

REX. Uh-huh! I know. You were re-enacting a very old scene, one of those that only the actors enjoy. But listen, big boy! Papa Larry's sure burnt up with you.

ROMEO. (*Helplessly to* CONNIE) What does he mean?

REX. Oh, I forgot you have to have an interpreter. Larry's got you behind the eight ball.

ROMEO. (*Still more bewildered*) Eight ball?

REX. You know; he's in a stew. He's boiling.

ROMEO. (*Alarmed*) You mean he fell into a stewpot? My! It must have been a large one.

REX. (*Disgusted*) Oh, Mammy! Listen! Why did you have to come down here with that great big story about you being a scientist?

ROMEO. (*Offended*) I beg your pardon! I never stated I was a scientist. My accounts of scientific achievement were based solely upon the successes of my late Uncle Benvolio.

REX. You sure put up some bluff with that A-B-C-D bomb.

CONNIE. That's just the point, Rex, he wasn't bluffing.

REX. (*Startled*) You mean it's as good as he says it is?

CONNIE. It's not that kind of a bomb.

ROMEO. (*Disconsolately*) I must confess that I am bitterly disappointed in it because I thought it was Uncle Benvolio's A-B-C-D bomb. Actually it is his virus exterminator.

CONNIE. When it is discharged it instantly purifies the air for yards and yards around and it will cure any disease that is caused by virus. And it will also cure a common cold like that! (*Snaps her fingers.*) He let me smell a little of the gas used and it cured a touch of cold I had instantly.

REX. (*Incredulously*) You mean you proved it, Connie?

CONNIE. (*With conviction*) I certainly have.

ROMEO. I can assure you it is exceedingly efficacious.

REX. (*Excitedly*) Then where are those furniture movers? We're rich! We're billionaires! Yes, trillionaires, even quadrillionaires! (*Studies an instant.*) My gosh! We might even make a million out of it! (*Races to door* R.) Larry! Come here quick!

BILLIE. (*Dashes in* R.) What in the world's the matter with you?

REX. Nothing! We got the dough!

BILLIE. (*Disgustedly*) It's about time you waked up. I could have told you all along but you wouldn't listen.

REX. Does everyone know about this but me?

BILLIE. No, darling! You and I are the only ones who know unless you told Connie and Romeo.

REX. Unless *I* told them? *They* told *me!*

BILLIE. How could they tell you when I'm the only one who's seen the paper?

REX. What paper?

BILLIE. About the accident, silly!

REX. (*Aghast*) Oh, the accident. I'd forgotten for the time being. Let me outta here before she serves me with another one. (*Starts* L.)

BILLIE. (*Grabs and holds him*) Darling! You're going to get $2,000 out of it.

REX. (*Struggling to get free*) I can't do it. Where in the world am I gonna get two thousand smackeroos? Lemme go!

BILLIE. From the accident, foolish.

REX. But I tell you I haven't got —— (*Stops.*) *I'm gonna get $2,000?*

BILLIE. Yes, you get $2,000—and me!

REX. H-h-how come?

BILLIE. (LARRY *and* ORPHA *appear in door* R.) Pulling that rich man out of the car was the bravest thing I ever heard of. And it was perfectly wonderful of you, darling, to pick a rich man to save. (*Tries to hug him.*) Darling!

LARRY. I'm sorry for the way I yelled at you, Rex. The insurance girl was just telling us about you. That surely was a brave act—pulling that man out of the burning car. Incidentally, your having that money can save our furniture. Shall we bring it back in?

REX. (*Gulping*) You—you wouldn't believe me, I suppose, if I told you when we cracked up I had the top down and smashed plumb into the side of the other car and he had his window rolled down and I kept right on going, through the window and into his lap. You wouldn't believe that, would you?

ALL. (*Laughing among themselves*) Of course not! We believe that? I should say not. Isn't he a card! (*Etc.*)

REX. When the car caught fire and I started to get out,

that man grabbed right onto me and held on and I just couldn't shake him off and that's how I saved him. But I suppose you won't believe that either?

ALL. Of course not. Why, Rex! How you carry on. How could we believe that? Such a fantastic story. A hero and trying to get out of it. (*Etc.*)

REX. (*With a sigh of relief*) Well, my conscience is clear. Boy, can I enjoy that two thousand now, but wait until you hear what our little backwoods Romeo has got.

LARRY. (*Grimly*) I don't want to hear any more about *that*. I know all about it.

REX. You mean you know about him having a bomb that you can set off and it will clear every cold within so many yards?

LARRY. (*Incredulously*) What!

CONNIE. It's true, Larry. It really works. I tried it.

LARRY. You're sure?

CONNIE. Positive!

LARRY. Whoopee! That does it! (*Grabs* ORPHA *and whirls her about.*) Who said we couldn't find a scientist?

REX. Whoopee! (*Starts to grab* BILLIE *but stops.*) Do you mind?

BILLIE. I'd love it!

REX. (*Taking her gingerly by the shoulders*) Let's start off easy so if you change your mind I can duck and run. (*Whirls her easily and seriously, then very joy- fully.*) YIPPEE!

(ROMEO *watches the boys for an instant, then looks at* CONNIE.)

LARRY. Go ahead, Romie! She won't bite!

CONNIE. Come on, Romeo. Let's show them we're not afraid.

REX. I'll show you. (*Grabs* BILLIE *and illustrates.*) Put your arms around her like this and then do this! (*Puts arms around* BILLIE *and kisses her lightly on the forehead.*)

ROMEO. (*Disappointed*) You call *that* a kiss?

REX. That, my backwoods Romeo, is a kiss.

ROMEO.   (*Reproachfully to* CONNIE)   You were in error.

LARRY.   (*Laughing*)   You mean that Connie ——

CONNIE.   (*Embarrassed*)   Now hush, all of you.

REX.   (*Mischievously*)   Show us what *she* told you, Romie.

ROMEO.   I would rather not, but if it was wrong the mistake should be rectified. (*Steps up to* CONNIE, *puts his arm around her and kisses her on the forehead.*) Ohhhh! "Get thee behind me, Satan." "Get thee behind ——" (*Kisses* CONNIE *on the lips.*)

(*All laugh.* ROMEO *breaks with* CONNIE *and looks around more or less dazed.* CONNIE *glares them into silence.*)

CONNIE.   (*To* ROMEO)   Well! Which do you like best? Rex's right way or your wrong way?

ROMEO.   (*To* LARRY *and* REX)   Have either of you tried *my* way?

REX *and* LARRY.   No, but we will. (*Together they turn to their girls and kiss them, then turn to* ROMEO *and laugh heartily.*)

ROMEO.   (*Very much pleased with himself, speaks to* CONNIE)   Do you know, I believe *we* have perfected something new. (*He looks much bewildered as all laugh.*)

QUICK CURTAIN

MURDER AT THE GREY'S HOUND MANSION
Maxine Holmgren

Mystery, High School/ Community Theatre /5f, 3m/ Simple Set
This is a mysterious comedy (or a comical mystery) that will have everyone howling with laughter.

The eccentric owner of Grey's Hound Mansion has been murdered. The cast gathers at the gloomy mansion for the reading of the will. Lightning lights up the stage as thunder and barking dogs greet the wacky characters that arrive. Each one is a suspect, and each one suspects another. Mixed metaphors and alliterations will have the audience barking up the wrong tree until the mystery is solved.

Baker's Plays
7611 Sunset Blvd.
Los Angeles, CA 90046
Phone: 323-876-0579
Fax: 323-876-5482

BAKERSPLAYS.COM

STONE SOUP
Anne Glasner & Betty Hollinger

Musical, TYA/Children's Theatre / 9m, 7f, 2 either / Simple Set
2 hungry soldiers stumble on a town filled with disgruntled neighbors. Using their imaginations, the soldiers trick the townsfolk into donating seasonings for their legendary Stone Soup, which they have convinced the townsfolk is a delicacy beyond measure. They con the townfolk into giving them all the ingredients to make a real soup, and in doing so, the soldiers help the townsfolk learn how to get along with each other by working together to create something good.

Baker's Plays
7611 Sunset Blvd.
Los Angeles, CA 90046
Phone: 323-876-0579
Fax: 323-876-5482

BAKERSPLAYS.COM

ELEANOR FOR PRESIDENT
Merritt Ierley

18+ m, 9+ f, ensemble (some gender flexibility and doubling possible)
A woman as Chief Executive? The 2008 presidential campaign proved it possible, yet it just might have happened more than half a century earlier. Eleanor Roosevelt, First Lady from 1933 to 1945, might have run for president after the death of her husband, Franklin. Many thought about it, some talked about it, a few actually suggested it. That Eleanor Roosevelt did not seek public office was of her own choosing, and chiefly her own priorities as well as a sense that the time was not yet right. Act I of Eleanor for President briefly scans her career to a point where she might have run. Act II fictionalizes the fork in the road not takes. The net result is a unique, sometimes witty, and always insightful look at Eleanor Roosevelt and the political process.

Baker's Plays
7611 Sunset Blvd.
Los Angeles, CA 90046
Phone: 323-876-0579
Fax: 323-876-5482

BAKERSPLAYS.COM

www.ingramcontent.com/pod-product-compliance
Lightning Source LLC
Chambersburg PA
CBHW070638120726

47909CB00004B/1490